KU-650-436

REUNITED
BY A BABY
BOMBSHELL

BY

BARBARA HANNAY

Metropolitan Borough of Stockport
Libraries

003122836   509

MILLS
BOON

All rights reserved including the right of reproduction in whole or in part in any form. This edition is published by arrangement with Harlequin Books S.A.

This is a work of fiction. Names, characters, places, locations and incidents are purely fictional and bear no relationship to any real life individuals, living or dead, or to any actual places, business establishments, locations, events or incidents. Any resemblance is entirely coincidental.

This book is sold subject to the condition that it shall not, by way of trade or otherwise, be lent, resold, hired out or otherwise circulated without the prior consent of the publisher in any form of binding or cover other than that in which it is published and without a similar condition including this condition being imposed on the subsequent purchaser.

® and TM are trademarks owned and used by the trademark owner and/or its licensee. Trademarks marked with ® are registered with the United Kingdom Patent Office and/or the Office for Harmonisation in the Internal Market and in other countries.

First published in Great Britain 2017
By Mills & Boon, an imprint of HarperCollins*Publishers*
1 London Bridge Street, London, SE1 9GF

Large Print edition 2017

© 2017 Barbara Hannay

ISBN: 978-0-263-07128-3

Our policy is to use papers that are natural, renewable and recyclable products and made from wood grown in sustainable forests. The logging and manufacturing processes conform to the legal environmental regulations of the country of origin.

Printed and bound in Great Britain
by CPI Antony Rowe, Chippenham, Wiltshire

REUNITED
BY A BABY
BOMBSHELL

CHAPTER ONE

WHEN THE INVITATION arrived Eva Hennessey was away in Prague, dancing the role of Odette in *Swan Lake*. On her return to Paris a week later, she found her mailbox crammed, mostly with an assortment of bills and dance magazines. She was riding the rickety old lift to her apartment on the fifth floor when the bright sunny Australian stamp caught her eye. Then she read the postmark. Emerald Bay.

The sharp pang in her chest made her gasp. It wasn't homesickness. Eva's feelings about the beach town where she'd grown up were far more complicated. These days, she rarely allowed herself to unpack the mixed bag of emotions that accompanied memories from her youth.

She always ended up thinking about Griffin

Fletcher…and the other harrowing memory that would never leave her.

She'd worked hard to put that life behind her. She'd *had* to. Long ago.

Today, as the hum of Parisian traffic reached Eva from the street below, she let herself into the apartment that had been her home for the past ten years. Nanette, the concierge, had already turned on the heating and the apartment was welcoming and warm. Eva had loved this place from the day she'd first found it.

Decorated simply in quiet creamy tones with occasional touches of blue, the main living area was dominated by a far wall of windows that looked out over tiled rooftops, chimneys and church spires to the top of the Eiffel Tower. At night, on the hour, the Tower glittered with beautiful lights. It was a view Eva never tired of.

Stopping for a moment, she smiled to herself as she looked about the space she'd carefully assembled over the years—the beautiful cushion covers she'd picked up on various tours, the collection of blue and white pottery from all over Europe, the wide-brimmed bowl full of shells and stones she'd collected from beaches in Greece and Italy, in Spain and the UK. So many happy memories to counteract the sad ones from her past.

She set down her luggage and dumped the envelope from Australia on the coffee table along with the rest of her mail. Then she went through to the bathroom and had a long hot shower, massaging the nagging pain in her hip under the steady stream of water.

She washed her hair, dried it roughly with a towel, letting the damp dark tresses hang loose past her shoulders as she changed into a comfy pair of stretch slacks and an oversized T-shirt.

Soon she would make her supper. A simple herb omelette would suffice. But first a glass of wine, an indulgence she could allow herself now that the performance tour was behind her.

Curled on the sofa, with the wine within reach and a cushion positioned to support her painful hip, Eva retrieved the envelope from Australia and slit it open. A card depicting an iconic Queensland beach fell out.

Beneath the picture, a message—an invitation to a reunion of her classmates to celebrate twenty years since their last year of high school.

Eva felt sick as she read the details.

Where: Emerald Bay Golf Club
When: Saturday October 20th

The simple wording hit her like a punch to the chest. A thousand long-suppressed images crashed in. The beach in summer and the thrill of riding the rolling green surf. The smooth trunk of a palm tree at her back as she sat at the edge of the sand, eating salty fish and chips wrapped in paper. The smell of sunscreen and citronella.

Her thoughts flashed to hot summer days in classrooms with windows opened wide to catch a sea breeze. And then, despite her best efforts to block them, there were memories of Griffin Fletcher.

Griff, sitting at the desk just behind her in

class, all shaggy-haired and wide-shouldered, catching her eye when she turned and sending her a cheeky grin.

Griff on the football field. The flash of his solid thighs as he sped past to score a try.

Griff holding her close in the dark. The surprising gentleness of his lips.

And, flashing between those sweeter memories, the fear and the crushing weight of her terrible secret. The overwhelming heartbreak and pain.

Enough.

Stop it.

Eva knew at once what her response would be. What it *must* be. Of course she couldn't possibly go. With deep regret, she would be unable to accept the kind invitation. She was very grateful to be remembered by her old school friends, but her schedule was far too tight.

It wasn't untrue. She had a new set of rehearsals for *The Nutcracker* lined up and she couldn't really afford the time away. And why would she want to go back to the Bay anyway? Her mother no longer lived there. It was many years now since her mum had married and settled in Cairns in the far north of the state. As for Eva's classmates and the rest of her memories—of necessity, she'd very deliberately left all that behind.

Instead, she'd worked as hard as possible for those twenty years, putting in endless, punishing hours to build the career of her dreams. These days, posters of Eva Hennessey, dancing as Giselle, as Cinderella or as Romeo's Juliet, were on display in almost every theatre or train station in Europe.

After long years of hard work, this was Eva's reward. Rave reviews claimed her as 'technically poised and polished and lyrically perfect'. Wherever she went, audiences cheered *Bravo!* and gave her standing ovations. Her dressing rooms were crammed with beautiful flowers.

Eva's world was now different in every way imaginable from the life she'd known in the sleepy seaside town of her youth. She might as well be living on a different planet. If she ever returned to Emerald Bay, she would not only awaken past hurts, she would feel like an alien.

Just the same, she felt sick to the stomach as she tucked the card back into the envelope. She told herself she was simply overtired after the gruelling weeks on tour.

In the morning she would post an 'inability to accept' and she would delete all thoughts of Emerald Bay.

Bees buzzed in the bottlebrush hedge. Small children laughed and squealed as they splashed at the shallow end of the elegant swimming pool, while their mothers watched, dangling their bare legs in the water as they sipped Pimm's from long glasses. The smell of frying onions floated on the balmiest of breezes. It was a typical Sunday afternoon in suburban Brisbane.

Griff Fletcher was the host on this particular Sunday and his guests were a couple of long-time mates and their families. Griff was repaying their hospitality while his girlfriend, Amanda, was away in Sydney on business. It made sense. Amanda hadn't known these guys for decades as he had. They weren't really part of her scene—she was so much younger than their wives—and she didn't 'do' little kids.

As Griff added steaks to the sizzling barbecue plate, the men helped themselves to fresh beers and kept him company.

'So what do you reckon about the school reunion?' asked Tim, who, like Griff, had moved from Emerald Bay to live and work in Queensland's capital city. 'Are you planning to check it out, Griff?'

Griff shrugged. He'd known that Tim and Barney were bound to talk about the reunion today, but he really wasn't that interested. 'I think I might give it a miss,' he said.

Tim pulled a face, clearly disappointed. 'But surely you must be curious about your old mates? Wouldn't you like to catch up with the gang?'

The best Griff could manage was a crooked grin. 'I see you two often enough.'

Barney gave an awkward smile and Tim scowled and took a long drink of his beer. Griff scowled too, as he began to flip steaks. He knew it wouldn't be long before one of the guys had another dig at him.

Tim shook his head. 'I know you're a hotshot barrister, Griff, but I didn't take you for a snob.'

Griff gave another shrug as he turned the sausages for the children. 'I just don't see the point in revisiting the past. You know what these reunions are like. The only people who turn up are the ones who've been successful, or the ones who've bred a swag of offspring. Then they swan around feeling smug, gossiping about the ones who stayed away.'

'That's a bit harsh,' Tim said stiffly.

'I wasn't talking about you of course, mate.'

His mate wasn't mollified. 'Have you ever been to a school reunion?'

'No, but it's easy to—'

'I have,' cut in Barney. 'My folks still live in the Bay, so I'm up there pretty regularly and I went to the ten-year reunion.' He looked a tad defensive. 'I enjoyed meeting up with everyone again, even after just ten years. There were some who'd really changed and others who looked exactly the same. Not that any of that mattered. We all had plenty of laughs and swapped war stories. It was interesting to hear what everyone's doing.'

'See!' crowed Tim with a triumphant grin.

Griff shrugged again and used the egg flip to shift the browned onions away from the heat. Then he turned to call to the women. 'Steaks won't be long.'

'Right,' Tim's wife, Kylie, called back. 'We'd better get these kids dry then.'

Tim, meanwhile, moved closer to Griff. Out of the corner of his mouth, he said, 'Eva Hennessey's not likely to be there.'

Griff stiffened, and was immediately annoyed that the mere mention of Eva could still raise a reaction. It really shouldn't matter if he ran into a girl he'd known a million years ago.

The reaction didn't make sense. Sure, Eva had been his first girlfriend, but he'd eventually got over the shock of her leaving town so abruptly. It wasn't as if he'd been planning to marry her straight out of high school and settle down in the Bay. He'd had big plans for his future.

He'd carried on with his life, with university and his subsequent career. And in the past two decades he'd had more than his fair share of relationships with glamorous, beautiful, passionate women.

He supposed it didn't really make sense that he wanted to avoid Eva, but he'd moved on, so why ask for trouble?

'Of course she won't be there,' he said, pleased that he managed to sound offhand. He added another nonchalant shrug for good measure, but he bit back the other comment that had sprung to mind—that Eva Hennessey was far too busy and world-famous to come back for such a piddling, unimportant event.

'Well, Barney's already put his name down, haven't you, Barnes?' Tim called to their mate, who was retrieving an inflatable ball that had bounced out of the pool.

Barney sent them a thumbs up.

'And I reckon it'd be a blast for the three of us

to go back to the Bay,' Tim persisted. 'You know, just the Three Amigos, without the women and billy-lids. Like the good old days.'

Griff was about to respond in the negative, but Tim stopped him with a raised hand.

'Just think about it, Griff. We could stay at a pub on the beachfront, catch a few waves, even do a little snorkelling and diving on the reef.'

Well, yeah.

Griff couldn't deny the great times he and these mates had enjoyed as teenagers, lapping up the free and easy outdoor lifestyle of a bay-side country town.

Griff's family had moved back to the city as soon as he'd finished school, and he could barely remember the last time he'd donned goggles and flippers to dive into the secret underwater world of coral and fish.

But there'd been a time when he'd lived and breathed diving…and surfing. Throughout his teenage years, he'd spent a part of every single day at the beach, in the sea. And every night, in bed, he'd listened to the sound of the surf pounding on the sand. The rhythm of the sea had been as familiar and essential to him as the beating of his heart.

By contrast, these days, the only water he saw was when he was rowing on the Brisbane River, which was usually flat and brown and still.

But the sea was different. And the Bay was special.

More to the point, these two mates were important to Griff. Amanda wasn't especially fond of them, but she did have a tendency to be slightly snooty. She preferred mixing with Griff's barrister colleagues and their partners, whereas Griff knew that these guys kept him grounded. Tim worked in a bank and Barney was an electrician and, between them, they provided a good balance to the eminent judges and silks who filled Griff's working life.

He'd be crazy to let the haunting memory of one slim, dark-haired girl with astonishing aqua eyes spoil the chance to go back and recapture a little of the camaraderie and magic he'd enjoyed in his youth.

'I'll think about it,' he said cautiously.

He was rewarded with a hearty and enthusiastic back-slap.

Eva stared at the doctor in dismay as two words echoed in her head like a tolling funeral bell... Hip replacement...hip replacement...

It was the worst possible news. She couldn't take it in. She didn't want to believe it.

A few days earlier, during a rehearsal of *The Nutcracker*, she'd landed awkwardly after performing a *grand jeté*, a demanding movement that involved propelling herself gracefully into the air and doing the splits while above the ground. Eva had performed the move thousands of times, of course, but this time, when she'd landed, the pain in her hip had been agonising.

Since then, the hip hadn't improved. She'd stayed away from rehearsals, claiming a heavy cold, which was something she'd never done before. Normally, Eva danced through every painful mishap. She'd danced on broken toes, through colds and flu, had even performed for weeks with a torn ligament in her shoulder.

Such stoicism wasn't unusual in ballet circles. A culture of secrecy about injury was a given. Every dancer was terrified of being branded as *fragile.* They all understood it was a euphemism for *on the way out*—the end of a career.

This time, however, Eva found it too difficult to keep hiding her pain. Even if she faked her way through class and rehearsals, by the time she got home she could barely walk. So she'd seen an osteopath. But now, to her horror, the doctor had shown her disturbing results from her MRI scan.

She'd never dreamed the damage could be so bad.

'You've torn the labrum,' the doctor told her solemnly as he pointed to the scan. 'That's the ring of cartilage around your left hip joint. Normally, the labrum helps with shock absorption and lubrication of the joint, but now—' He shook his head. 'The tear on its own wouldn't be such a great problem, but there are other degenerative changes as well.' He waved his hand over the scan. 'Extensive arthritic inflammation of the whole joint.'

Arthritis? A chill washed over Eva. Wasn't that something that happened to elderly people?

'I strongly recommend a complete hip replacement. Otherwise—' the doctor sighed expressively '—I don't really see how you can avoid it.'

No, please no.

On a page from his writing pad, he wrote the names of two consultant orthopaedic and trauma surgeons. He handed the paper to Eva.

Sweat broke out on her skin and she swayed a little dizzily in her chair. A hip replacement was a death knell, the end of her career. The prospect filled her with such desolation that it didn't bear imagining.

It would be the end of my life.

'Aren't there other things I can try?' she asked in desperation. 'Besides surgery?'

The doctor gave a shrug. 'We can talk about physiotherapy and painkillers and diet. And rest,' he added, giving her a dark look. 'But I think you'll find that the pain will still be too severe, certainly if you want to continue dancing. Ballet requires movements that are very unnatural.'

Eva knew this all too well, of course. She'd spent a lifetime perfecting the demanding movements most people never even tried. Pirouettes and adagios and grand allegros *en pointe* all made exacting demands on her limbs and joints, and she knew she was only human. She was at the wrong end of her thirties and there was a limit to what she could expect from her body. But she couldn't give up dancing.

Not yet! She'd worked too hard, had sacrificed too much. Sure, she'd known that her career couldn't last for ever, but she'd hoped for at least five more years.

Dancing was her life. Without it, she would drown, would completely lose her identity.

She was in no way ready for this.

The osteopath was staring at her a little impatiently now. He had no more advice to offer.

In a daze, Eva rose from her chair, thanked him and bade him goodbye. As the door to his office closed behind her, she walked through reception without seeing anyone, trying not to limp, to prove to herself that the doctor must have been wrong, but even walking was painful.

Glass doors led to a long empty corridor. What could she do now?

She tried to think clearly, but her mind kept spinning. If she gave in and had the surgery, she was sure the company wouldn't want her back—certainly not as their prima ballerina—and she couldn't conscience the idea of going back into the corps de ballet.

The worst of it was, this wasn't a problem she dared discuss with her colleagues. She didn't want anyone in the dancing world to know. The news would spread like wildfire. It would be in the press by lunchtime. By supper time, her career would be over.

As she made her way carefully down a short flight of stairs and onto the Parisian pavement outside, Eva, who had always been strong and independent, valuing her privacy, had never felt more vulnerable and alone. On the wrong side of the world.

'Hello, this is Jane. How can I help you?'

Griff grimaced. He couldn't believe he was tense about speaking to Jane Simpson. In their school days, Jane had been the Emerald Bay baker's daughter. Since then she'd married a cane farmer and was now convening the class reunion.

'Hi, there, Jane.' He cleared his throat nervously and was immediately annoyed with himself. 'Griff Fletcher, here. I'm ringing about the school reunion weekend.'

'Oh, yes.' Jane sounded excited. 'It's great to hear from you after all this time, Griff. I hope you'll be able to come.'

'Well, I'm still trying to see if I can...er...fit it into my schedule. But I was curious—how are the...er...numbers shaping up?'

'They're great, actually. We have about thirty-five coming so far—and that's not counting partners. It's really exciting,' Jane enthused. 'I do hope you can make it.'

'Yeah, thanks.'

Since the barbecue with Tim and Barney, Griff had been warming to the idea of going back to the Bay. But he wanted to ask about Eva. The thought of running into her in front of everyone from their school days completely ruined the picture. There was too much unfinished business between them. There was bound to be tension. And friction. It would be unavoidable.

If Eva was going to be there—which Griff very much doubted—he would stay well clear of the place.

The simple question should have been easy to put to Jane. Griff couldn't believe he was uptight.

It wasn't as if he'd spent the past twenty years pining for his high school sweetheart. Many of the relationships he'd enjoyed since then had been fabulously passionate and borderline serious.

Admittedly, Griff's relationships did have a

habit of petering out. While almost all of his friends and colleagues had tied the knot and were starting families, Griff didn't seem to have the staying power. He either tired of his girlfriends, or they got tired of waiting for him to commit to something more permanent.

At least he and Amanda were still hanging together. So far.

Now, he braced himself to get to the point of this phone call. Every day in court he faced criminals, judges and juries, and he prided himself on posing the most searching and intimate of questions. It should be a cinch to ask Jane Simpson a quick, straightforward question about Eva.

'I don't suppose...' Griff began and stopped, as memories of Eva's smile flashed before him. The view of her pale neck as she'd leaned over her books in class. The fresh taste of her kisses. Her slim, lithe body pressing temptingly close.

'Have you heard from Eva?' Jane asked, mercifully cutting into his thoughts.

Jane had been one of Eva's closest friends at

school, so she knew that he and Eva had once been an item.

Griff grabbed the opening now offered. 'No, I haven't heard from her in ages. We're…not in contact these days. Has she been in touch with you?'

'Yes, and I'm afraid she's not coming,' Jane said. 'It's such a pity she can't make it.'

OK. So now he knew without having to ask. Relief and disappointment slugged Griff in equal parts.

'I'm not at all surprised,' he said.

'No, I'm sure Eva's incredibly busy with her dancing. It's wonderful how amazingly well she's done, though, isn't it?'

'Yes—amazing.'

'Anyway, Griff, let me know if you do decide you can come. It should be a fun get-together. Do you have my email address?'

Jane dictated the address while Griff jotted it down. He would leave it a few days before he emailed her. In the meantime, he would swing by Tim's favourite lunching hangout and let him know he was free to join him and Barney on a nostalgic trip back to their schoolboy haunts. And if he did happen to see Eva again, of course he wouldn't lose his cool.

Eva sat beneath the red awning of a pavement café, clutching a cup of blissfully decadent hot chocolate as she watched the rainy Paris streetscape. Beyond the awning's protection, raindrops danced in little splashes in the gutter. Across the street, the lights of another café glowed, yellow beacons of warmth in the bleak grey day.

Even in the rain Paris looked beautiful but, for the first time in ages, Eva felt like a tourist rather than a resident. She could no longer dance here and everything had changed.

She'd come to Paris to work, to further her career. Until now she'd been a professional with a full and busy life. Her days had a rhythm—limbering and stretching, promotions and interviews, rehearsals and performances.

If she lost all that, what would she do?

She hadn't felt this low since she'd broken up with Vasily, her Russian boyfriend, who had left her for a lovely blonde dancer from the Netherlands.

Such a dreadful blow that had been.

For eight years, Eva had loved good-looking Vasily Stepanov and his sinfully magnificent body. They had danced together and lived and loved together, and she had looked on him as her partner in every sense. Her dancing had never been more assured, more sensitive. Her life had never been happier.

She'd learned to cook Vasily's favourite Russian dishes—borsch and blini and potato salad with crunchy pickles, and she'd put up with his outbursts of temper. She'd even taken classes to learn his language, and she'd hoped they would marry, have a baby or two.

Getting over him had been the second hardest lesson of her life—after that other terrible lesson in her distant past. But now the devastating news about her hip was an even worse blow for Eva.

Sipping her rich, thick *chocolat chaud*, watching car tyres swish past on the shiny wet street, she found herself longing for sunshine and she remembered how easily the sun was taken for granted in Australia. A beat later, she was remembering the beach at Emerald Bay, the smooth curve of sand and the frothy blue and white surf.

And, out of nowhere, came the sudden suggestion that it made perfect sense to go back home to Australia for her surgery.

She could ask for leave from the company. Pierre was already rehearsing a new Clara for *The Nutcracker*, and the understudy was shaping up well. Eva was, to all intents and purposes, free. She found herself smiling at the prospect of going home.

She would make up some excuse about needing to see her mother. It wasn't a total lie. It was years since she'd taken extended leave and it was at least two years since she'd been home, and her mum wasn't getting any younger. If she had the surgery in an Australian city hospital, she'd have a much better chance of flying under the radar than she would here in ballet-mad Paris.

There might even be a chance—just a minuscule chance—that she could come back here to Paris as good as new. She'd been researching on the Internet and had read about a leading dancer in America who was performing again after a hip replacement. The girl was younger than Eva, but still, the story had given her hope.

And, Eva thought, as she drained the last of the creamy rich chocolate, if she was returning to Australia, she might as well go to that school reunion. She'd had an email from Jane Simpson telling her that Griff was undecided so, if she went, she was unlikely to have the ordeal of facing him.

She would love to catch up with everyone else. It felt suddenly important to her to chat with people who lived 'normal' lives.

Yes, she decided. She would go.

As soon as this thought was born, Eva was hit by a burst of exhilaration. This was swiftly followed by a shiver of fear when she thought about Griff, but she shook it off.

It was time to be positive and brave about her future. Perhaps it was also time to lay to rest the ghosts of her past.

CHAPTER TWO

THE BAY HAD changed a great deal. Griff and Tim were surprised and impressed by the new suburbs and shopping centres that had sprung up in their home town. The school was almost unrecognisable, with a host of extra buildings, including a big new gymnasium and performing arts centre.

At least the fish and chip shop looked much the same, painted white with a blue trim and with big blue pots spilling with red geraniums. And the natural features of sea, sky and beach were as alluring as ever. Now, though, smart cafés graced the prime spots along the seafront, and there were neatly mown parks with landscaped gardens.

The guys remembered paddocks of prickly bindi-eye weeds that they'd had to run across to get to the beach, but now there were very civilised paved walking paths, and carefully planted vines crawled over the sand dunes to hold them in place.

Nevertheless, the three friends had a great afternoon trying to recapture the fun of their youth, falling off surfboards, getting sunburnt, donning snorkels, goggles and flippers to explore the striped and colourful fish and coral on the inshore reefs that rimmed the headland.

Griff was certainly glad that he'd come. It was refreshing to spend some quality time with friends whose links stretched way back. Despite his high-powered job, or perhaps because of it, he'd lately found himself going to too many dinner parties and concerts with the same snooty circle, rehashing the same old conversations, the same narrow views of politics, the same tired jokes.

Now, as the sun slid towards the west, washing the sky with a bright pink blush that lent gold tints to the sea, the trio returned to their hotel to shower and change for the reunion.

Griff, changed into pale chinos and a white open-necked shirt with long sleeves rolled back to the elbows, checked his phone, half expecting a message from Amanda, even though they'd broken up. He was sure she would be still keeping tabs on him. She'd had plenty to say about his 'boys' weekend'.

They'd had another row, of course. He'd accused her of not trusting him. She'd claimed she would trust him if he put a ring on her finger.

In the end, she'd walked out and the next day she'd sent a taxi to collect her belongings.

Unfortunately, she wasn't the first girlfriend to leave in this manner, but his love life was a hassle Griff didn't want to think about now. After an afternoon of sun, sea and mateship, he was feeling more relaxed than he had in ages. He wanted to keep it that way.

The trio were crossing the wide stretch of mown lawn in front the Emerald Bay Golf Club when Griff came to a sudden halt, as if he'd slammed into an invisible glass wall.

He'd caught just the merest glimpse of a slim, dark-haired woman on the side balcony overlooking the golf course and he'd known immediately that it was Eva.

Hell, she wasn't supposed to be here.

But here she was—wearing a sleeveless white dress, and laughing and chatting with a group. Even at a distance, Griff recognised her. No other woman was so slim and toned and poised. No one else had such perfect deportment, was so naturally elegant.

Hell. Now Griff knew he'd been fooling himself. His confidence that he could see Eva again and remain indifferent was shattered.

He was back in the past, remembering it all— helping her to adjust a pair of goggles and then teaching her to skin dive, helping her with her maths homework, dancing with her at the school formal. She'd worn a long silky dress in an aqua colour that exactly matched her eyes, and she'd made him feel like a prince.

He'd been saving for a surfboard, but he'd spent all his carefully hoarded pocket money on Eva's birthday, buying her an aquamarine pendant on a silver chain.

'What's the matter, Griff?' Barney's voice intruded his thoughts.

Both Tim and Barney were staring at him.

'Nothing,' Griff responded quickly.

The guys frowned at him, then shrugged and walked on. Griff, grim-faced, kept pace with them.

Hell. He gave himself a mental shakedown. Of course he could do this. He was used to hiding his feelings. He did it every day in court. Sure, he could play the role of an old friend, who'd barely given his high school sweetheart a second thought during the past twenty years. Sure, he could grit his teeth and sweat this scene out. For an entire weekend.

Jane had only warned Eva at the very last minute that Griff was coming. Actually, Jane hadn't couched the news as a warning. She had passed it on in high excitement, certain that Eva would be totally delighted.

By then, Eva had already arrived in the Bay and was settled into a pleasant motel room with ocean views, so it had been too late to change her mind. Just the same, when Jane shared this news, Eva found it devilish hard to grin and pretend to be pleased.

'He's not bringing his girlfriend, though,' Jane had added.

The existence of a girlfriend was good news at least. The possibility that Griff was still single and at a loose end had bothered Eva for all sorts of ridiculous reasons. Instead, he was safely in a relationship, which meant there were no loose ends.

Great. Their past was a closed door and that was how it would remain.

Eva had told herself she was stupid to fret. After all these years, Griff would have forgotten all about her. There was absolutely no reason he'd still be interested. After she'd left town, he'd studied for years at university and since then he'd been fighting the good fight in the justice system. Griffin Fletcher was a top drawer barrister these days, totally brilliant. Such a lofty and noble pursuit.

No doubt he would look down on a ballerina who spent her days pirouetting and leaping about, and see her as someone fluffy and inconsequential.

At least Eva was used to keeping her emotions under wraps and remaining composed in public, and now, with the reunion well underway, she tried to ignore any stirrings of tension as she chatted with old school friends. Everyone was eager to hear all about her dancing career and her life in Europe, but she tried to keep her story low-key.

She was keen to hear about their lives as accountants and teachers, as nurses and farmers, and she was more than happy to look at their photographs of their adorable kids.

She was exclaiming over a photo of Rose Gardner's six-month-old identical twins when she heard Jane's voice lift with excitement.

'Oh, hi, Barney and Tim. Hi, Griff.'

Griff.

Despite her calming self-talk, Eva's heart took off like a runaway thief. Unhelpfully, she turned Griff's way, which wasn't wise, but the instinct was too powerful to resist.

She thought she was well prepared for her first sight of him, but in a moment she knew that was nonsense. She was trembling like the last leaf on an autumn branch.

There he was. A man who would stand out in any crowd. Probably no taller than before, but certainly broader across the shoulders and chest. Still with the same shaggy brown hair, the same rugged cheekbones, the slightly crooked nose and square, shadowed jaw. The same intelligent grey eyes that missed nothing.

Not quite handsome, Griff Fletcher was undeniably masculine. There were perpendicular grooves down his cheeks that hadn't been there at eighteen, and he'd lost his easy, boyish smile. Now he had the air of a gladiator about to do battle, and Eva felt as if she might burst into flames.

'Griff,' Jane was gushing, 'how lovely to see

you again.' A beat later, too soon, 'Isn't it wonderful that Eva was able to join us after all?'

With a beaming smile, Jane turned to Eva and beckoned. 'I told Griff that you weren't coming.' She giggled, as if this were an enormous joke.

Eva saw the fierce blaze in Griff's eyes. It wasn't a glare, exactly, but she got the distinct impression that he would definitely have stayed away if he'd known she would be here.

Thud.

She desperately wanted to flee, but she forced herself to stand her ground and to dredge up a smile. This became easier when she shifted her gaze from Griff to his old schoolmates, Tim and Barney.

Barney had grown round and was losing his hair, but his blue eyes twinkled and his smile was genuine and welcoming. 'Hey, Eva,' he said. 'Great to see you again.' He clasped her hand and gave her a friendly kiss on her cheek. 'I'm going to have to get your autograph for my daughter, Sophie. She's just started to learn ballet.'

'How lovely. Good for Sophie.' Eva gave Barney her smiling, super-focused attention. 'How many children do you have now?'

'Two and a half. A boy and a girl, with another on the way.'

'Barney's working on having enough kids to field a football team,' commented Tim as he shot his mate a cheeky grin.

Eva laughed. 'I hope your wife's in on that plan, Barney.'

Tim gave her a kiss, too. He told her that he worked in a bank and that he and his wife had just one child at this point, a little boy of two called Sam.

All too soon, it was Griff's turn to greet Eva and the light-hearted atmosphere noticeably chilled, as if someone had flicked a switch. The sudden tension was palpable—in everyone—in Tim and Barney and herself. Eva's heart was beating so loudly she feared they must hear it.

Griff smiled at her. It was a tilted, lopsided effort, but to the bystanders it probably passed as affable and casual. Eva, however, saw the expression in his eyes. Cold. Unfathomable. Cutting.

'How are you, Eva?' He went through the motions, giving her a casual hug and a peck on the cheek.

Ridiculously, her skin flamed at the contact, and she lost her breath as his big hands touched her shoulders, as his arms brushed, warm and solid, against her bare skin. Then his lips delivered a devastating, split-second flash of fire.

She took a moment to recover, to remember that she was supposed to answer his simple question. *How are you, Eva?*

'I'm very well, thanks, Griff.' Thank heavens she was able to speak calmly, but she hadn't told him the truth. She wasn't feeling well at all. She felt sick and scared—scared about the secrets she'd never shared with this man, that she'd hoped she would never have to share.

And her hip was agony. She'd foolishly, in a fit of vanity, worn high heels, and now she was paying the price. She prayed that she didn't blush as Griff's glittering grey gaze remained concentrated on her.

'And how are you?' she remembered to ask.

'Fighting fit, thank you.'

With the conventions over, an awkward silence fell. Tim and Barney looked at their shoes, and then at each other.

'We should grab a drink,' Tim said.

'Sure,' Barney agreed with obvious enthusiasm. They both turned to head for the bar, seeming keen to get away. 'Catch you two later.'

Griff remained still, watching Eva in stony silence and making her feel like one of his guilty criminals in the dock. This time her face flamed and she knew he could see it.

'You haven't changed,' he said quietly.

She shook her head. Of course she'd changed. They'd all changed in so many ways, both on the outside and, undoubtedly, within. But she played the game. 'Neither have you, Griff. Not really.'

At this, his smile almost reached his eyes.

She wondered if he was about to say something conciliatory. It would be helpful to at least share a few pleasantries to bridge the wide chasm of years. Of silence.

And guilty secrets.

'I hear you've been very successful,' he said. 'You're world-famous now. Congratulations.'

Receiving this praise from Griff, delivered in such a chilling tone, she wanted to cry.

But she swallowed the burning lump in her throat, squared her shoulders and lifted her chin. 'You've been very successful, too.'

He responded with the merest nod and only the very faintest trace of a smile. 'I imagine we've both worked hard.'

'Yes.'

People all around them were chatting and laughing, waving and calling greetings, sharing hugs, enjoying themselves immensely, but Eva couldn't think of anything else to say.

Griff said, 'If you'll excuse me, Eva, I'll head over to the bar and grab a drink, too.'

'Of course.'

'I'm sure we'll run into each other again during the weekend.'

'I...I...yes, I'm sure.'

With another nod, he dismissed her. As he moved away, she felt horribly deserted, as if she'd been left alone on a stage with a spotlight shining on her so everyone could see her. She could almost hear the music that accompanied *The Dying Swan*, the sad notes of a lone cello.

Oh, for heaven's sake.

Eva blinked and looked around her. The reunion was gathering steam. The balcony and the large dining room inside the clubhouse were almost full now with chattering, happy people and no one was staring at her.

She drifted, clutching her warming glass of champagne. She looked at the corkboard covered with old photographs. There were class photos, sporting teams, the senior formal, the school camp on Fraser Island. She saw a photo of herself in the netball team, Griff and his mates in striped football jerseys and shorts. Another photo showed her in a ballet tutu and pointe shoes, performing a solo for the school concert.

The old photographs conjured memories— the school disco when she and Griff danced together for the very first time, the dates when he'd taken her to the movies and they'd snogged each other senseless in the popcorn-scented dark, the barbecue for his eighteenth, the bonfire on the beach. And afterwards...

The memories were beyond painful and the urge to cry wouldn't go away.

'Would you like something to eat?'

Eva turned. A young girl was offering her a tray laden with canapés.

'Prosciutto crostini with dried cherries and goats' cheese,' the girl said. 'Or potato cakes with smoked salmon.'

Eva wasn't hungry, but she took a potato cake. Anything was better than staring miserably at those photos. She even managed to smile at the girl, who was rather interesting-looking, with dark hair cut into a trendy asymmetrical style. She had a silver nose stud as well, and there were purple streaks in the long fringe of hair that hung low, framing one side of her pretty heart-shaped face.

The girl returned Eva's smile. 'You might like a napkin.' She nodded to the small pile on one side of her tray.

'Thanks,' Eva said.

The girl was staring at Eva and there was something intriguing, almost familiar, about her clear grey eyes. 'You're Eva Hennessey,' the girl said. 'The ballet dancer.'

'Yes, that's right.'

The girl's eyes widened. 'Wow,' she said. 'You live in Paris, don't you? How amazing to meet you.'

Eva smiled, feeling calmer. This was familiar ground. 'It's great to be back in Australia,' she said. 'Are you from the Bay?'

The girl gave a small laugh that might have been nervous. 'Kinda. But I'm studying at university in Brisbane now.' Then she must have realised she was spending too long in one place. 'Better get going,' she said, and she hurried away to offer the platter to a nearby group.

Before long, Eva was absorbed into another group of schoolmates and was once again fielding friendly questions or listening to their stories about their old teachers, about their jobs, their kids or their holidays in New Zealand or Bali.

It was easy enough to avoid Griff and she was beginning to relax a little and to enjoy herself once more. If she and Griff kept apart by mutual agreement, the evening might be manageable after all.

Griff was feeling calmer as he stood in a group by the bar. Half his old rugby league team were gathered there and the guys were having a great old time sharing memories—the game when Tony King broke his leg while scoring a try, or the year they won the regional premiership by a whisker, when Jonno Briggs kicked a freakish field goal.

The whole time, though, Griff was all too aware of Eva's presence, even though she was at the far end of the room with her back to him. He did his damnedest to stop looking her way, but it was as if he had special radar beaming back sensory messages about her every move.

'Would you like something to eat, sir?'

A girl arrived, offering canapés.

'Thanks.' The savouries looked appetising. Griff smiled. 'I might take two.'

The girl laughed and there was a flash in her eyes, a tilt to her smile—something that felt uncannily familiar. For a moment longer than was necessary, the girl's gaze stayed on Griff, almost as if she were studying him. Fine hairs lifted on the back of his neck.

The feeling was unsettling and he might have said something, but then she turned and began serving the others. She didn't look Griff's way again and he decided he must have been more on edge about the whole Eva business than he'd realised.

He would be glad when this night was over.

Dinner was about to be served and everyone settled at long tables. Eva sat with some old girlfriends and their husbands. Griff was two tables away, almost out of sight, and she did her best to stop her gaze from stealing in his direction. She was relatively successful, but twice he caught her sending a furtive glance his way. Both times he looked angry and she felt her cheeks heat brightly.

'Are you all right, Eva?' asked Jane, who was sitting opposite her.

'Yes, of course.' Eva knew she must look flushed and she reached for her water glass. 'Just feeling the heat.'

Jane nodded sympathetically. 'It must be hard for you, coming back from a lovely cool autumn in Europe to the start of a sweltering summer in Queensland.'

'Yes,' Eva said. 'You tend to forget about the heat and just remember the lovely sunshine.'

Others around her nodded in agreement or laughed politely.

As they finished their main course, speeches were made. Jonno Briggs, who'd gone on after school to become a professional footballer, told a funny story about running into Barney in a pub in Glasgow. Jane gave a touching speech about one of their classmates who had died.

There were tributes to a couple of their old teachers who had also returned for the reunion.

Then someone decided to point out their most successful classmates and Eva, among others, was asked to stand. As she did so, somewhat reluctantly, there was a burst of loud applause.

'Give us a pirouette, Eva!' called Barney.

She winced inwardly, remembering the way she'd liked to show off when she was still at school. So many times she'd performed arabesques and grand jetés on the beach.

'I couldn't possibly,' she told them now.

'Oh, come on!' called a jocular fellow at the back.

'Sorry. My dress is too tight.'

This was accepted with good-natured laughter.

At least she didn't have to mention the flaring pain in her hip. She would prefer no one knew about that.

The desserts arrived. Eva was served by the girl with the purple-streaked hair who had chatted to her earlier. She gave Eva an especially bright smile and a sly wink, as if they were great mates.

Eva usually avoided desserts and she only ate

half of her *crème brulée*. With the speeches over, people were rising from their seats and starting to mingle again. There was self-serve coffee at one end of the bar and Eva crossed the room to collect a cup.

'We should talk,' a deep voice said at her elbow.

Griff's voice. Eva almost spilled her coffee.

His expression was serious. Determined. Eva supposed he was going to grill her, ply her with questions. She was rather afraid of that clever lawyer's mind of his. Would he try to uncover her secret?

A flood of terror made her tremble. When she turned his way, she did so slowly, hoping to appear unruffled. 'What would you like to talk about?'

Griff's cool smile warned her not to play games. 'I suspect we'd both benefit from laying a few ghosts.'

She couldn't think how to respond to this. 'I... guess.'

'Let's go outside. You can bring your coffee with you.'

Eva was struggling with her hip and the high heels and she didn't trust herself to carry a cup of hot liquid. 'I'd prefer to drink it here.'

His expression remained unruffled. 'As you wish. There's no rush.'

'Well, no, I guess not.' In an attempt to banish her nervousness, she tried for lightness. 'Not after twenty years.'

But with Griff standing there, waiting for their 'talk', she was suddenly so tense the coffee curdled in her stomach. After three sips she set the cup down.

He frowned. 'You're finished?'

'Yes, thanks. Where would you like to go?'

He nodded towards a pair of glass doors that led to another, smaller, balcony. 'We should have more privacy out there.'

Privacy with this man. *Great.* Just what she didn't need, but she knew she shouldn't refuse him. From the moment she'd decided to come back to the Bay, she'd been aware that this encounter was a possibility.

Perhaps it was time.

If only she felt ready.

As Griff opened the door for her to precede him, the only light on the balcony came from an almost full moon. They were facing the sea now and a breeze brought a flurry of salty spray. The moon shone over the surf, highlighting the silvery curl of the waves and the white froth of foam as it crashed on the pale sand.

Eva gripped the balcony railing, grateful for its support. Now, in the moonlit darkness, Griff seemed to loom larger than ever.

'So,' she said, turning bravely to face him. 'What would you like to discuss?'

'I'm sure you must know, Eva. Perhaps you're hoping that after twenty years I'd simply overlook the way we broke up, but I'm afraid I'd like to know why you took off like that.'

She nodded, drew a deep breath. Of course she'd guessed this would be Griff's question and she knew she must tell him the truth. If only it wasn't so difficult, after all this time. When they were young they'd been able to talk endlessly, with an easy, trusting intimacy that would be impossible now. They'd shared everything.

Well, *almost* everything.

Now, they were virtually strangers.

She was tempted to use her mother as her excuse, but that would be cowardly. Although it *had* been her mum's idea to take off, leaving no word.

'I know you, Eva,' her mother had said on that fateful night before they'd left Emerald Bay under cover of darkness, as Eva had wept and begged to go to Griff. 'Be sensible, darling. If you try to explain what we're doing, you'll end up telling him everything. He might make demands and it will become way too complicated.'

Eva had tried to protest, but her mother had insisted. 'You need to make a clean break now. You have to think of your dancing career. You have so much promise, darling. Everybody says so—your teacher, the examiners, the Eisteddfod judges. You can't throw that away. I won't let you.'

There had been tears in her mother's eyes. Eva's potential career was incredibly important to her. She'd started dressing Eva in ballet tutus when she was three years old. By the time she was eighteen, Eva's ballet career had probably been more important to Lizzie Hennessey than it had been to Eva.

It was only much later, with the benefit of distance and maturity, that Eva had understood that her struggling single mother had been desperate to ensure that her daughter wasn't trapped and held back, as she had been.

Eva hadn't allowed herself to question whether she'd been wrong to listen to her mother. Of necessity, she'd clung to the belief that she had done the right thing. And her career had repaid her a thousandfold.

The wind swept her hair over her face. With shaking fingers, she brushed it away. 'I know it was bad of us to take off like that,' she told Griff. 'I've always felt guilty about it.'

'You were my first girlfriend,' he said. 'But you were also the first girl to dump me.' He sounded less aggressive, closer to the friendly Griff of old. 'I admit my ego took a blow.'

He stepped up to the railing, standing beside her now, with his hands deep in his trouser pockets as he looked out to sea. Eva could see his profile: his broad, intelligent forehead, his strong nose, his lips that she'd once explored with such excitement and daring.

'I thought I must have upset you,' he said quietly. 'We were both virgins. At the time, you seemed keen. I know you were keen, but I've often wondered if...I don't know...if I'd scared you.'

Oh, Griff, never. Tears stung Eva's eyes. 'That wasn't the problem, honestly. It was—'

'Excuse me.'

A voice brought them both swinging round. It was a girl—the waitress with the purple streaks in her hair.

Had she been sent to summon them inside?

Eva wasn't sure if she was annoyed or relieved by the interruption.

'What is it?' Griff snapped, making his own reaction quite clear.

'I was hoping to speak to you both,' the girl said, but she seemed less confident now. She was wearing a white shirt and black skirt and she fiddled with the buckle at her waist.

Eva glanced Griff's way and saw his eyes narrow as he frowned at the girl. 'Well?' he demanded impatiently.

'I wanted to introduce myself.' Her grey eyes were huge with an emotion that might have been overwhelming excitement or fear. 'You see,' she added, lifting her hands from her sides, palms facing up in a gesture that was both nervous and helpless, 'I'm your daughter.'

CHAPTER THREE

G<small>RIFF FELT AS</small> if he'd been king-hit, knocked to the ground, left in a gutter, bruised and battered. He stared at the girl in appalled disbelief. Surely he hadn't heard her correctly.

Their daughter?

Impossible.

And yet, as he slowly gathered his wits, he had to ask himself if this wasn't also entirely possible. He'd used precautions back then, but heaven knew he'd been inexperienced and overexcited at the time. *Hell.* There was evidence enough in what had followed—Eva's rapid departure and silence.

And now, twenty years later, this creature, this attractive young woman, tall and dark-haired, with clear pale skin and shiny grey eyes and an air of familiarity that had nagged at Griff from the moment he'd seen her.

Their daughter?

Emotions tumbled through him like the pounding surf. Shock. Anger. Sadness. Regret. And then another thumping wave of anger.

All this time, all these years—Eva had kept their child a secret? His first impulse now was to round on her, to demand a full explanation.

A quick glance Eva's way, however, showed her sagged against the railing, white and trembling, possibly even more shocked than he was. Unfortunately, she wasn't denying the girl's claim.

'I'm sorry,' the girl said. 'I know this must be a huge surprise. A shock, I expect. But I was so anxious to meet you both. That's why I took this waitressing job as soon as I heard about the reunion. I was so excited when I saw the list of names and realised that you were both going to be here.'

Dazed, Griff rubbed at his temple. Could this girl, this unique, vibrant being, really be an amalgam of his and Eva's genes? A life they'd created?

He still couldn't quite believe he was a father. He didn't want to believe he'd been a father all this time. *Bloody hell.*

A thousand questions demanded answers, but he wasn't prepared to expose his total ignorance in front of the girl. At this point, there was no way of verifying her outrageous claim.

'What's your name?' Eva asked in a whisper, while she kept a white-knuckled grip on the railing, as if it were the only thing keeping her upright.

'Laine,' the girl said. 'That's the name you gave me, isn't it? Laine Elizabeth?'

Tears shone in Eva's eyes as she gave a sad, slow nod. 'Yes,' she said and, with a single syllable, she answered Griff's biggest question.

'I'm Laine Templeton now,' the girl said. 'Or sometimes Lettie to my closest friends, because my initials are L.E.T. The people who adopted me—the Templetons—live in Brisbane.'

'And they told you about me?' Eva sent a frightened glance Griff's way. 'About...us?'

Laine shook her head. 'No, I didn't want to upset them, so I went straight to the adoption agency. I'm over eighteen, so I was perfectly entitled to find out the names of my birth parents.' Her gaze met Griff's. 'I'm studying law at UQ. I was intrigued to look you up on the Internet and discover you're a barrister.'

Griff felt as if he'd swallowed glass. He supposed he should feel some kind of fatherly connection to this girl. He wanted to feel sympathy for Eva, but he was too busy dealing with his own roiling emotions.

Eva shouldn't have kept this from him. She shouldn't have carried this burden alone. Damn it, she should have shared the news of her pregnancy.

Sure, they'd been young at the time, only just out of school, and both of them with big career dreams with absolutely no plans to start a family. He hadn't been anywhere near ready for parenthood, but it cut deep to realise he'd been denied the chance to face up to this challenge, to at least be part of the decision-making.

'Look, I know this is a bolt out of the blue,' Laine said, and she was already taking a step backwards as she looked carefully from Griff to Eva. 'I just wanted to introduce myself initially, but I guess you need time to…adjust.'

'Yes, we do,' Griff told her more sternly than he'd meant to.

She smiled shyly, awkwardly.

'I'm sorry,' Eva said through trembling lips. 'I…I…'

Clearly, Eva was struggling to say anything coherent.

Laine lifted her hand then and gave a shy, shining-eyed smile and a stiff wave. 'OK,' she said. 'I dare say my timing hasn't been great.'

Griff felt torn. This was his daughter, after all. It felt totally inadequate to just greet her with *Hi and 'bye*. But he was too shocked to think straight. 'Look, this really is a shock,' he said. Maybe—'

Eva spoke up. 'Maybe tomorrow.'

'Yes, sure,' said Laine. 'I'm sorry if I've upset you. I…I…'

'We can at least exchange contact details tomorrow,' Griff suggested. That would be a start, and about all they could manage under the circumstances. Eva looked as if she was about to collapse.

'Thanks,' said Laine. 'I'll see you then.'

She backed away quickly and as she left via the glass doors Eva opened her mouth as if she wanted to say goodbye, but no sound emerged and she looked as if she was about to collapse.

Griff stepped towards Eva again, torn between wanting to tear strips off her and feeling desperately sorry for her. What must it be like for a mother to be reunited with her baby after nineteen long years?

'Are you OK?' he asked.

Eva shook her head. 'Not really.'

She was still clinging to the railing as if it were a life raft. Clearly, she needed to sit down and Griff was wondering where he could take her so that they could be private.

'Would you mind walking me back to my motel?' Eva asked, as if her mind had been on a similar track.

It was the perfect option. 'No, of course not.'

Griff slipped his arm around Eva's shoulders. He felt the softness of her bare skin, sensed the supple strength of her slender frame, toned by years of dancing. But now he knew that her magnificent career had come with a huge price tag. He wasn't sure he could forgive her.

It was a relief to lean into Griff's massive shoulder and to have his strong arm firmly around her as they walked the short distance across the lawn to the beachfront motel where Eva was staying.

She should have been terribly self-conscious about this sudden proximity to the man she'd avoided for so many years, but now her thoughts were filled to the brim with Laine. For so long, that beautiful girl had lived in Eva's head and heart as a tiny newborn.

Such a shock to see her baby now. Out of the blue. So astonishingly alive and grown-up and beautiful, and wanting to get to know her and Griff.

And Griff. She still hadn't come to terms with seeing him again. In one night, the love of her life and the daughter she had given up were both suddenly back in her life. It was too much. Too unreal. Too overwhelming.

Eva couldn't quite take it all in. She'd never felt such see-sawing emotions, teetering between joy and sorrow and guilt. Huge guilt.

'There hasn't been a day when I haven't thought about her, haven't wondered.' She only realised she'd spoken this out loud when she felt Griff's arm tighten around her.

He didn't say anything, however, and Eva couldn't imagine what he must be thinking. He would be terribly angry with her of course.

Keeping secrets was dangerous. They were usually exposed sooner or later, and the longer the secret was kept in the dark, the more likely it was that people would be hurt. Deeply hurt.

Would Griff ever forgive her?

* * *

It wasn't long before they reached the motel. Griff dropped his arm from Eva's shoulders and she fished in her bag for the room key.

'Would you like to come in?' she asked him, knowing she couldn't reasonably send him away like this, with so many unasked and unanswered questions.

'Yes, of course. We need to talk.'

Eva nodded, pushed the door open and slipped the key-card into the slot that turned on the lights. The motel room was large and comfortable, with a small sitting area comprising a couple of armchairs, a coffee table and a shaded table lamp.

She quickly switched off the lamps by the king-sized bed. A silly reaction, no doubt, but she didn't want to draw attention to the seductive banks of pillows, the soft throw rug arranged artistically across the grey silk quilt. She kicked off her shoes. Her hip was screaming and for a moment she had no choice but to stand there with her eyes closed, massaging the inflamed joint with her thumb.

Ah, that was better.

When she opened her eyes, she saw Griff watching her, his gaze narrowed, his expression concerned.

She smiled weakly. 'I think I'm getting too old for high heels.'

He shook his head in obvious disbelief and Eva quickly changed the subject. 'I'm sure you could do with a drink, Griff.' She crossed the room and checked out the minibar. 'What would you like? I seem to have it all here—Scotch, gin, rum, beer, red or white wine, champagne.'

'I'm sure I need a Scotch.'

'With water? Ice?'

'A little ice.'

He didn't say please, which probably meant he was angry, and he remained silent, seeming to fill the motel room with his dark and brooding presence as Eva poured the contents of the small bottle into a glass, found the ice cubes in the fridge's tiny freezer and twisted them free to tumble with a soft clink.

She emptied a packet of nuts into a small green dish and set them on the glass coffee table in front of him.

'Thanks,' he said as she handed him the drink. 'You'll join me, won't you?'

Eva doubted that anything could soothe her shaken nerves tonight, but she opted for white wine. With her glass filled, she took the seat opposite Griff, surreptitiously arranging a cushion to support her hip.

Griff, by contrast, looked surprisingly at ease, lounging in his pale chinos with an ankle propped on a knee. Distractingly attractive too, with his white shirt open at the throat, the sleeves rolled back to reveal muscular forearms, and his thick, longish hair curling boyishly at the ends.

Lifting his glass in a salute, he smiled, but his smile was a complicated mix of sadness and caution. 'Cheers. I guess I should say: Here's to our daughter.'

Our daughter.

The words were like splinters pressing into Eva's heart. She thought again of Laine as a tiny baby, thought of the years of gut-wrenching loss and longing, of not knowing, and her mouth pulled out of shape. She had to press a fist to her lips to hold back the threat of tears.

Not now. He will hate it if I cry.

To her relief, she managed, with a supreme effort, to compose herself.

'Laine's beautiful, isn't she?' she couldn't help saying.

'She is, yes.' Griff took a deep swallow of his Scotch and regarded Eva sternly. 'And you owe me one hell of an explanation.'

'I know.' She set her glass down without even bothering to taste the wine. Her hand was shaking and a little of the wine spilled, but she didn't get up to find something to wipe it. Neither of them needed another delay. 'I guess you realise now why I left the Bay in such a hurry.'

'I put two and two together, yes, but I have no idea why you chose to leave me in the dark.'

Griff's eyes were fierce as he glared at her. 'I had a right to know that I'd fathered a child.'

'Yes, Griff. I know. I'm sorry.' It was hard to think clearly under his vigilant scrutiny. Eva dropped her gaze to the serviceable grey carpet. 'I do feel bad about it.'

'So why did you lock me out?'

Eva swallowed nervously, knowing that her excuse didn't sound nearly as valid now as it had seemed at the time. 'Do you remember the debate in our English class, when you argued in favour of abortion?'

A kind of strangled gasp broke from Griff. 'Not especially—there were so many debates. But don't tell me—' He stopped, clearly shocked.

'You were so clever and persuasive, Griff. Putting your case so strongly, slashing every argument the opposition tried to put up. Even at school you already sounded like a brilliant lawyer. And you made abortion sound so logical and sensible.'

'But it was a debate, for God's sake.' Griff was staring at her now in total disbelief. 'Eva,

I was handed the topic. I didn't choose which side to take. You know how those school debates worked.'

'Yes, but at the time I had just found out I was pregnant and I couldn't help feeling that you were speaking to me, telling me that abortion was the right choice, the only sensible choice.'

He gave an angry shake of his head. 'I can't even remember the damned debate, but the argument would have been purely theoretical. I might have been persuasive. I'd have wanted our team to win. But you must know that's not necessarily how I would have reacted in a real life situation.'

'Well, yes, I know that now.' Eva sighed, recognising how frustrating this must be for him. 'And I suppose I sort of guessed it at the time, but you were so convincing, Griff. And I wanted to keep the baby—or at least I wanted it to be born, to have a life. I was scared that if I told you I was pregnant, you might want me to get rid of it and I wouldn't be clever enough to argue my case.'

She expected Griff to protest, but his eyes were so round with concern that she found it hard to breathe.

When he didn't say anything, she pushed on, needing him to understand. 'I was already under a lot of pressure from my mother. She was very keen for me to have a termination. She'd been a single mum and she knew how hard it could be. She wanted everything to be so much better for me. And she was so worried I would ruin my chances of ever becoming a dancer.'

'Well, I'm sure that was a distinct possibility,' Griff said. 'Weren't you auditioning for the Australian Ballet at the time?'

Eva nodded. 'For the Aussie Ballet *School*. I'd been through the regional auditions and I'd been selected for the finals in Melbourne. It was a huge deal for me—and for Mum. Oh, my God, Mum was beside herself with excitement.'

'Did you go to Melbourne?'

She shook her head. 'There was no point. I was going to have a baby.'

Griff swallowed, looked distressed. Then he

frowned and stared pensively at the distant wall, as if he needed to take a good long time before he spoke. Watching him, Eva thought this might be how a judge might look in court, as he weighed up the evidence before he announced his sentence.

'So now your choice has been vindicated,' he said at last. 'You've had a brilliant career and you've been able to see that your baby has grown into a healthy and bright young woman.'

'Yes.' Eva swallowed the horrible lump in her throat. The results weren't as perfect as Griff made them sound. She had made these decisions with the best of intentions but, by keeping Laine a secret from him and then handing her over for adoption, three lives had been scarred for ever.

'I do apologise for not telling you,' she said. It was on the tip of her tongue to add that giving him up had been as hard for her as giving up her baby. Her heart had been broken twice over. But it was rather too late to mention romantic feelings from twenty years ago. She could imagine Griff's disbelieving laugh. 'I've always felt guilty about keeping the pregnancy a secret,' she said instead.

He sighed, looked at his glass again, then took another hefty swig of Scotch. As he set it down, he met her gaze directly.

'What happened after you left here? If you didn't go to Melbourne, where did you go instead?'

'To Bowen.'

'Bowen?' He looked shocked. Bowen was a small town a thousand kilometres away in north Queensland.

'It was quiet up there,' she said. 'No one knew us. The locals weren't likely to gossip or spread rumours, so Mum and I could stay under the radar. Mum got a job in a fish and chip shop. I spent a few months helping at the local ballet school, until I got too huge.'

'So Laine was born in Bowen?'

'No, we came down to Brisbane for the last month of the pregnancy. She was born in the Royal Brisbane and Women's Hospital. The adoption was already arranged.'

Eva said this as quickly and matter-of-factly as she could, and then looked away, staring hard at the opposite wall, willing herself not to cry. She didn't add that she'd almost tried to find Griff in Brisbane when the baby was about to be born. There was no point in telling him now that she'd come so close to seeking him out at university, hoping for one last, desperate chance.

At the time, she'd still been weaving foolish fantasies about the two of them raising the baby together, with Griff at university during the day and her working in ballet schools in the evenings. She'd imagined that, between them, they might have sorted something out. But, in the end, despite the allure of these dreams, she hadn't gone to Griff.

After so many months, she hadn't been brave enough to land such a last-minute bombshell at his feet. After all, he hadn't come after her when she'd left. He could have followed her, found her. He would have done if he'd really cared. Never mind that she'd handed him a terrible rejection, given him no reason to believe such an approach would be successful. He still could have followed her. Hollow as the thought was, she'd tried to cling onto it. It was all she'd had.

He frowned. 'You must have had to work incredibly hard to get yourself fit again after the baby. The ballet scene is so competitive. Were you still able to go to Melbourne?'

'No, I'd missed that chance. Mum and I moved to Sydney and I signed up with a suburban ballet school, just to get back into shape. But, while I was there, I went to workshops with the professional companies whenever I could and I met a visiting choreographer from the Netherlands. He encouraged me to head for Europe. He told me to audition with companies everywhere. He was sure I would find a home.'

Griff pulled a face. 'I suppose that must have been good advice. It's certainly worked well for you, but didn't you feel terribly young to just head off like that?'

'I was almost twenty and I'd had a baby. I felt very grown-up.'

He acknowledged this with a rueful quarter-smile.

'I've been with four or five different companies in Europe,' Eva said, keen to finish her story. 'But I've stayed with the one company in Paris for the last ten years.'

'As their star, their prima ballerina.'

'Not at first, but yes, eventually.'

With her story now off her chest, Eva felt calmer. She drank a little of her wine, while Griff remained silent as if he was digesting everything that she'd told him. She wondered if he would grill her further about her decision to keep the baby a secret. Or would he leave now? He had the bare essentials and there was little point in chatting away into the night like old friends.

'You never married,' he said suddenly.

It was almost an accusation and Eva felt the impact like a slap.

Defensively, she sat a little straighter, tucked a wing of dark hair behind her ear. 'No, I haven't.'

'It can't have been for lack of offers.'

She felt her cheeks grow warm, but she was too proud to tell Griff about her eight years with Vasily, and the subsequent painful dumping, so she held her tongue.

'I suppose you haven't had time for marriage,' Griff suggested drily. 'You've been too busy touring.'

'Well, yes, it's a gypsy life, being on stage.'

His eyes glimmered with the merest hint of amusement. 'A gypsy? What kind of caravan do you have?'

'An apartment in Paris. I love it, actually. In the seventh *arrondissement.*'

Griff looked impressed, gave a nod of approval.

'Have you been there?' she asked.

'In the Eiffel Tower district? Yes, of course.'

This was another small shock to add to the many Eva had received this evening. She wondered when Griff had been in Paris. He must have been within a mere block or two, possibly metres from her home. Could they have passed in the street? Missed each other by moments? The possibilities made her eyes sting.

She blinked hard. So many years…they'd drifted so far apart, and yet she could still remember everything about their youth. The fun of swimming and diving with Griff, the long walks over the headland, the secret trysts behind the dunes.

Was Griff remembering all of this, too?

In the silence, Eva grabbed the chance to ask him a careful question of her own. 'You have a partner, I believe?'

One of Griff's dark eyebrows hiked high. 'Who told you that?'

'Jane Simpson.'

'Ah, yes, Jane. She's an unreliable source, you know.'

'Why do you say that? Because she told you I wasn't coming to the reunion?'

Griff downed the last of his drink. 'That and also the fact that Amanda and I have split up.'

Eva gulped as she stared at him. For a moment there, she'd almost been pleased about the split, before she remembered there was nothing to be pleased about. There was absolutely no chance that she and Griff would ever get together again.

But she couldn't help wondering what had gone wrong. She couldn't imagine why any girl would willingly leave Griff. 'I suppose you must have broken up recently then?'

'Yes.' He looked for a moment as if he was going to add more, but he must have changed his mind.

'That doesn't seem—' She stopped, confused, not quite sure what she was trying to say.

'Don't get yourself in a stew,' Griff told her. 'Amanda and I were already heading for the rocks and I think this reunion was the last straw.'

His candour surprised Eva and the realisation that Griff was no longer in a relationship had a strangely inappropriate effect on her breathing. 'I'm sorry.'

'Don't be,' he said calmly. 'I'm an old hand when it comes to ending relationships.'

This latest revelation sent a jolt through her. It made absolutely no sense. The Griff she knew was gorgeous, clever, easy to get on with. A perfect catch any woman would be lucky to snare.

She was remembering the powerful, fierce love that she'd once felt for him—the schoolgirl crush that had blossomed over their last summer into something huge.

Griff Fletcher had been an all-round star in the classroom and on the sporting field and yet he'd chosen her, Eva Hennessey, as his girlfriend, even though the only thing she'd been really good at was dancing.

She remembered the way Griff used to look at her, the way his intelligent grey eyes used to shimmer with unexpected emotion, letting her see straight into his heart. Perhaps it was the rawness of youth, but no one else, not even her mother or Vasily, had ever looked at her with such transparent and touchingly honest emotion.

Surely other women must have experienced the thrill of that passionate look? Surely they had been similarly smitten? Over the years, Eva had imagined a host of women throwing themselves at Griff's feet. She'd made herself quite sick at times, just thinking about Griff and everything she'd missed.

'I'm sure you must be tired.'

She jumped as his deep voice intruded into her thoughts. 'Yes, I suppose I must be. It's been a big day.'

'Huge,' Griff agreed. His face was tight, unhappy.

Eva felt as if they'd made little headway. 'What are we going to do about Laine?'

Griff frowned. 'Right now I don't feel in a fit state to make any kind of decision. I need to get my head around…everything.'

'Yes, of course.'

Griff rose from his chair. Eva stood too. In her bare feet, he seemed to tower over her, but she resisted the temptation to stand on tiptoe.

And now, as he looked at her, an emotion that might have been sorrow or tenderness, or a mixture of both, showed in his handsome face. 'I meant it when I said you hadn't changed, Eva.'

She looked at him, noticed the grooves beside his mouth, the crow's feet, the beginnings of grey in his thick, shaggy hair. But in every way that mattered he was still the handsome guy she'd once loved.

'I was honest too, when I said the same about you.'

He smiled, a silent *as if.*

Then he stepped closer, put his hands on her shoulders, clasping her gently.

Eva's heart juddered in her chest. Surely he wasn't going to kiss her? She held her breath as Griff remained mere inches from her, holding her in his silvery gaze, while the memories from their past circled around them like prowling ghosts.

Her throat felt so dry she swallowed and she knew that she wouldn't stop him if he did try to kiss her. He was Griff, after all.

He lifted a hand and touched her cheek, a soft brush of fingertips that reached deep inside her.

'Just for the record,' he said. 'I do understand how very much you loved your dancing, how important it was to you, and I think you made a very brave choice.'

Ohhh.

Eva was so relieved and grateful she could have hugged him, but before she could do anything Griff pressed a kiss to her forehead, then stepped quickly away and turned for the door.

'Sleep well,' he said over his shoulder, but there was a sarcastic edge to his voice now, an acknowledgement that neither of them was likely to sleep easily tonight. Then he left, letting the door click softly closed behind him.

CHAPTER FOUR

GRIFF'S EMOTIONS WERE rioting as he strode away from the motel. Until this evening he'd always considered himself to be pretty calm and clear-headed, but tonight that belief had been shattered. Tonight his brain had been well and truly fried. Hell, he'd actually come within a whisker of kissing Eva.

What the deuce had he been thinking?

As he reached the edge of the grassy parkland beside the beach, he stopped, hands sunk deep in his pockets, looking out to the breakers and, beyond them, to the smoother moonlit sea. He needed to collect his thoughts before he reached the hotel and encountered Tim and Barney. His mates knew he'd been with Eva and, while he was reasonably confident that they wouldn't grill him about it, he needed to have a story ready that did not include Laine.

He wasn't prepared to share the startling news about his daughter. He was still coming to terms with her existence, let alone everything else Eva had told him tonight.

He'd been on an emotional roller coaster, that was for sure, swinging from disbelief and anger to guilt and regret. And yet the whole time he'd been listening to Eva's story, he'd found himself watching her, drinking in the delicious remembered details. The lustrous sheen of her dark hair, the slender grace of her neck, her expressive hands, her gorgeous legs, her astonishingly beautiful eyes.

She was even lovelier now. There was an extra layer, a depth he found himself longing to get to know. But that didn't mean he had to say out loud that she was as lovely now as she'd ever been. He was actually annoyed to think that Eva still had some kind of hold over him. Anyone would think he was still eighteen.

I should have followed my damn instincts and stayed away from this place...

A gust of wind blew in from the sea, bringing with it the fresh tang of salt and seaweed. Griff watched the moon riding high in the night sky, trailing delicate clouds like scarves. It was right here, under this moon, on this beach, that he'd kissed Eva for the very first time.

He could still remember the feel of her in his arms, so soft and sexy, despite her toned and slender frame, and he could remember the way she'd laughed with surprise when he'd drawn her in close. The laughter had died when she realised his intentions.

He'd been scared she would refuse him. They were only friends at that point, part of the gang of kids who spent as much of their spare time as possible at the beach. They'd never even been on an actual date. But, miraculously, Eva had been as eager for a kiss as he was, letting her soft lips part to meet his and winding her arms around him, wriggling her hips against him, teasing him mercilessly.

'You make me feel all glittery,' she'd told him later that night.

'Glittery?'

'Yes, sparkling and tinkling. It's kind of a look and a sound and a feeling, all wrapped into one.'

If he hadn't already been in love with her, he'd become a complete and helpless goner in that moment.

And he and Eva had become such experts at kissing. Of course it wasn't long before they'd wanted more than kisses. A few more months had passed, though, before the fateful night Griff invited Eva back to his place, while his parents and sister were away in Brisbane.

Griff had prepared dinner—baked fish and potatoes with an avocado salad—with wine and half a dozen candles. It was such a big deal. He'd been desperate to impress.

Eva had grinned when she'd seen how much trouble he'd gone to. 'Gosh, Griff, you wouldn't be trying to seduce me, would you?'

Her light-hearted comment had brought his high hopes crashing about his feet. Clearly he'd gone overboard. He was an idiot. A total loser. Seduction was supposed to be subtle.

But then Eva had turned the tables on him by leaping into his arms. 'You didn't have to go to all this trouble, you know,' she said, nibbling at his ear. 'We've been seducing each other for weeks now and I can't wait a minute longer. Let's have dinner later.'

So it was much later by the time they had their meal. By then the food in the oven had all dried out and the salad was limp, but neither of them had minded.

Damn.

Griff gritted his teeth, angry that he was feeling so choked up over ancient history. What was the point of remembering such juvenile nonsense? There was nothing about their past that either he or Eva could change.

He wasn't even sure that they would want to.

What he needed to concentrate on now were the consequences presented to him this evening. A baby. A daughter, given up for adoption. The stark pain in Eva's face when she'd seen their child. His own huge feelings of isolation and loss.

If only he'd known. If only Eva had told him. He'd deserved to know.

And what would you have done? his conscience whispered.

It was a fair enough question.

Realistically, what would he have done at the age of eighteen? He and Eva had both been so young, scarcely out of school, both ambitious, with all their lives ahead of them. He hadn't been remotely ready to think about settling down, or facing parenthood, let alone lasting love or matrimony.

And yet he'd been hopelessly crazy about Eva, so chances were…

Dragging in a deep breath of sea air, Griff shook his head. It was way too late to trawl through what might have been. There was no point in harbouring regrets.

But what about now?

How was he going to handle this new situation? Laine, a lovely daughter, living in his city, studying law. The thought that she'd been living there all this time, without his knowledge, did his head in.

And Eva, as lovely and hauntingly bewitching as ever, sent his head spinning too, sent his heart taking flight.

He'd never felt so side-swiped. So torn. One minute he wanted to turn on his heel and head straight back to Eva's motel room, to pull her into his arms and taste those enticing lips of hers. To trace the shape of her lithe, tempting body with his hands. To unleash the longing that was raging inside him, driving him crazy.

Next minute he came to his senses and knew that he should just keep on walking. Now. Walk out of the Bay. All the way back to Brisbane.

And then, heaven help him, he was wanting Eva again. Wanting her desperately.

Damn it. He was in for a very long night.

Eva tossed and turned restlessly for most of the night. At three a.m. she got up to make a mug of camomile tea and to pace the motel room.

Haunted by Griff.

Seeing him again had rocked her to the core, lifting the lid on all her carefully bottled feelings and longings, reminding her of everything wonderful that she'd lost when she left him.

She'd been shocked by the storm that seeing Griff had wrought. It didn't make sense that she should feel this way. Anyone would think she'd travelled back in time, that she was eighteen again. Inexperienced. Unworldly. Swept away by one man.

And then, of all things, she'd seen Laine again on the very same night…

Such a shock. At first, Eva hadn't been sure she could survive it.

Every day of the past nineteen years, she had relived the moment when her baby was placed in her arms, warm and squirming within the tightly wrapped blanket. She'd remember Laine's damp, dark hair, her shiny little eyes and her intoxicating newborn smell, the little birthmark shaped like a butterfly on her left ankle.

Laine had been a strong little thing and had

fought free of the blanket, kicking to expose one little foot and to wave a tiny, tiny pink hand at Eva. A baby hello.

A deep, painful love had welled in Eva's chest, had burst into her throat in a noisy, heartbroken sob. Within moments, an officious nursing sister had taken her baby away.

'We can't have her upsetting you, dear.'

Eva's mum had been there and she'd hugged Eva hard and had assured her over and over that the adoption was for the best, but Eva couldn't be consoled. She'd cried so hard and so long that eventually they had made her take a pill. And then she'd slept.

She only saw Laine briefly, one more time, on the day she'd signed the papers.

They'd given her a photograph, but that was all she had. Over the years she'd tried to imagine Laine growing into a toddler, a cute little girl, a teenager. She'd longed to know details. What did she look like? Was she happy? Was she sporty and brainy like Griff, or was she more like herself, dreamy and artistic?

The anniversaries had been especially hard—Laine's birthday, Christmas, Mother's Day. Eva had coped the only way she could, by dancing from dawn until dark.

She'd consoled herself that all the advice had been right. She had done the right thing. Laine had gone to a good home, to parents who desperately wanted her and would give her a happy childhood. But Laine had been denied ever knowing her real parents. No matter how well she was cared for, at some deep level she must have known she'd been abandoned by her mother, the one person in the world who should have loved her most.

Eva wished she'd known at the age of eighteen that keeping a big secret like that from the man she loved would leave a painful crack in her soul. She'd been told the sense of loss would be temporary, but it wasn't. It stayed there.

Eva finally got to sleep again just after dawn, and she slept late. When she woke, she still felt lonely and scared. Useless.

It was so upsetting to feel this way, after working so hard to put it all behind her. In Paris, the ballet company she worked with adored her. Her life was predictable and orderly. Her work was satisfying and safe.

Now, she'd been back in Emerald Bay for less than twenty-four hours and already the mirage of her life as a dancing star had been stripped away to reveal her as a fraud. In every way that truly mattered Eva felt like a failure. The huge decisions she'd made for all the best reasons—leaving Griff and giving up Laine—no longer made sense.

And no amount of floor-pacing could ease her turmoil.

She was just stepping out of the shower when she heard the knock on her door.

Her first thought was that it must be Griff, and her heart was racing as she dried herself and pulled on the towelling robe that the motel supplied. She hurried to the door in bare feet.

And, indeed, Griff was standing on her doorstep.

He looked as tired as Eva felt and he hadn't shaved, but the dark stubble suited him, to a sinful degree. It went with his shaggy hair. And he was dressed in faded denim jeans and a loose white T-shirt that made him look like the Griff of old. Her high school surfie boyfriend.

Eva drew a deep breath. *Calm down. Just deal with whatever he has to say. Think of this as another performance.*

'I probably should have warned you I was coming over,' he said, obviously sensing her tension, and yet making no attempt to hide his curiosity as he took in her robe and damp, towel-dried hair.

Self-consciously, Eva tightened the knot on her robe's sash. 'How…how can I help you?'

'I don't know about you, but I've had a pretty grim night. There seems to be so much unfinished business. Can we talk?'

'Well, yes—'

'My head's all over the place. I need to talk

about Laine and—' Griff didn't fill in the rest of his sentence.

'Yes, of course.' Eva pressed a hand to the sudden aching pulse in her throat. 'Come in.' She opened the door wider and took a step back.

Griff only hesitated for half a second before entering her motel room yet again. Of course, he couldn't miss the rumpled sheets of the unmade bed, but he politely looked away. Not, however, before several hot flashes streaked through Eva. She felt ridiculously naked beneath the towelling robe.

'Take a seat,' she said nervously. 'Can you give me a moment to get dressed?'

'Of course.'

She would have to dress in the bathroom and she felt stupidly self-conscious as she collected her underwear from a drawer and snatched the most convenient item of clothing from the nearest hanger in the wardrobe.

'I'll fill the kettle from the bathroom tap and you might like to make us both a cup of coffee,' she said.

'Sure.'

Eva handed Griff the filled kettle and disappeared into the bathroom, without looking back to catch his expression.

She did, however, see the appreciative look in his eyes as she emerged scant minutes later in a halter-neck aqua sundress. It was silly the way warmth spread from her chest to her face. She hoped it didn't show.

At least, judging by the aroma filling the room, Griff had made a pot of good strong coffee.

'Thanks,' she said as he handed her a steaming mug, and she took a grateful sip. 'Mmm, I needed this.'

'Haven't you had breakfast?'

'No, I slept in, but this is good. Coffee's fine.' It wasn't all that long now till the reunion's farewell lunch and that was bound to be huge, Eva was sure.

She and Griff sat in chairs opposite each other, just as they had on the previous night. Unfortunately, Eva didn't feel any calmer now than she had then. She took another, deeper sip of coffee. 'So,' she said. 'We need to talk about Laine.'

'Yes.' Griff shifted in his chair as if he wasn't quite comfortable either. 'I imagine she might have had a bad a night too. It's not every day you front up to your long-lost parents.'

Eva nodded sadly. 'We should be talking to her. I spent half the night wishing I hadn't sent her away. The poor girl must be wondering what we think of her, how we're going to react going forward.'

Griff's face was stern. 'A public venue like a high school reunion isn't exactly the best setting for a highly charged personal revelation.'

'No.'

'The last thing any of us needs is to give the old school gossips something extra juicy to gab about.'

Eva felt compelled to defend her daughter. 'At least Laine had the sense to find us when we were on our own last night.'

'That's true.'

'It was just such a shock, though. I couldn't

think straight.' Eva clutched her coffee mug more tightly. Their gazes met. This morning, Griff gave no sign that he harboured anger or resentment about her secrecy, but it was she who looked away first. It wasn't just her guilt that bothered her. The silvery-grey shimmer in Griff's eyes had haunted her for twenty years, and now it made her feel hot in the cheeks, as if she was once again a shy schoolgirl with an enormous crush.

'Are you angry, Griff?' She forced herself to look his way.

'Yes,' he said, meeting her gaze squarely. 'Actually, I swing between anger and—' he shrugged '—and feeling sorry for you, I guess. It's doing my head in, to be honest.'

'I'm sorry.'

'Yeah, I know you're sorry. You don't have to keep saying it.'

Eva accepted this small reprimand with a rueful smile. 'Well, I'm worried about how Laine feels too. I...I hope she's not too angry with me—'

'I certainly didn't get that impression.' Griff shrugged. 'It might be just normal, healthy curiosity on her part.'

'Perhaps.' But Eva was again swamped with the too familiar memories of the tiny baby she'd given away. The strong little body wriggling inside the tight blanket. The tiny foot kicking, the hand waving.

She shivered.

'Are you all right?' Griff asked.

She shook her head. She was scared. Her arms were cold, despite the warmth of the day, and she rubbed at them. 'I don't want Laine to think she was the worst thing that ever happened to me.'

'Was she?' Griff asked sharply and Eva saw her own worry and pain mirrored in his eyes.

She couldn't tell him the truth, couldn't expose him to the depth of her pain. The adoption had been her decision and hers alone.

And if she allowed herself to relive those memories now, she would break down completely. The last thing Griff needed was a blubbering ex-girlfriend.

'I suppose we already made the most sensible suggestion last night and that is to give Laine our contact details,' she said, determined to be more positive and practical. 'Our phone numbers at least.' In truth, she longed to spend ages with her daughter, getting to know everything about her, but she would need to feel stronger. More composed.

'I'd certainly like to have more contact with Laine,' Griff agreed. 'I don't want my daughter to think that I don't care about her.'

My daughter.

Goosebumps broke out on Eva's arms as he said these two simple but oh, so significant words.

'No, I'd hate that too,' she said quickly, and then she took another deeper sip of her coffee, hoping for extra courage. It was important to remain practical. To give Griff space. 'I don't suppose there's any real need for us to see Laine together,' she said next. 'I mean— after today, we'll be going our separate ways again, won't we?'

'I dare say.' Griff's tone was dry and hard to read. Even so, it sent inappropriate tingles all over Eva's skin.

It was so unhelpful that she kept remembering him as her boyfriend. Dancing on the beach with him. His kisses. That perfect night so long ago. The meal he'd gone to so much trouble to prepare. The candles…

Stop it.

'So,' she pushed on bravely, 'I guess it's probably best if we make contact with Laine separately, in our own time.'

Griff nodded. Drained his coffee mug.

She supposed he would leave now.

'How are your parents?' she asked, suddenly desperate to keep him there for just a little longer.

Griff looked surprised by her question, but then he shrugged. 'They're fine. In the peak of condition, retired to Mount Tamborine in the Gold Coast hinterland.'

'That must be very nice. And your sister?' Eva remembered Griff's sister, Julia, as rather intimidatingly clever. Julia had been school captain when they'd been mere eighth graders and she'd scooped up all the awards on speech night.

'Julia's married with five kids at last count, and she's also a high court judge, would you believe?'

'Truly? As well as five children? How does she do it?'

'I have no idea. I don't think anyone knows, but there's been a procession of nannies and household help.' Griff smiled crookedly. 'She's the jewel in my father's crown.'

Eva could well imagine this. Griff's parents had always had high expectations for their children and, while Griff had done very well for himself, he'd lived in his sister's shadow.

Back in their school days, Griff's parents had never met Eva, the daughter of a hippie single mum. They certainly wouldn't have approved of her, which was possibly why Griff had escaped to the beach whenever he could.

'I've been thinking about how lucky we were to grow up here,' he said, looking out of the window to a view through palm trees of the golden stretch of beach. 'So much sunshine and fresh air and open space.'

'I know.' Eva had spent far too much time during the night lost in unhelpful memories of her life here at the Bay. 'No one ever worried about whether we were getting enough exercise.'

'The hard part was dragging us inside to study.'

They shared smiles but, to Eva's dismay, a smile from Griff was almost as dangerous now as it had been in her teens. She dropped her gaze to the coffee table between them and spotted the piece of weathered coral that she'd found on the beach yesterday.

She reached for it now. It was bleached snow-white by the sea and the sun, and she could run her thumb over the smooth ends that had once been sharp, pointy branches.

Griff noticed and raised a curious eyebrow. 'A souvenir?' he asked.

'Perhaps. I have a collection of stones and

shells I've found on various beaches around the world.'

'And you keep them in Paris?'

'Yes.'

He nodded thoughtfully. 'I'm sure you must love living in such a beautiful city.'

'Well, yes, I do. It's wonderful.' It was easy to wax lyrical about Paris and she was suddenly keen to justify her choice of living abroad. 'There's so much to love. The beautiful architecture, the gardens and parks, the food.'

'Oh, my God, the French food.' Griff rubbed his stomach and gave an exaggerated groan. 'And it's not just the food in the restaurants. There are all those amazing markets as well.'

'Yes, mountains of mushrooms in autumn. Amazing berries in spring and summer, lavender honey.'

'Not to mention *foie gras.*'

She laughed at his enthusiasm, remembering him as a teenager with a constant interest in food. 'And in Paris there's the bonus that you don't need a car,' she said. 'And I adore the flower stands. I can buy a beautiful bouquet for three euros!'

'Sounds like you've totally adapted to the city life then.'

'Well, yes, I have. You can never feel lonely in a city like Paris—even if you're sitting on your own in a bar.'

Griff shot her a sharp, questioning glance. 'Do you spend a lot of time on your own?'

Thud.

Eva winced as she realised she'd steered herself straight into that trap. But the sad truth was that since Vasily had left her she'd spent more time on her own than she would have liked, but she wasn't about to admit that now to this man.

'Not a *lot* of time,' she hedged. 'But I do like the fact that I can be comfortably on my own if I choose to.'

'And that's fair enough,' Griff said easily.

'What about your life in Brisbane?' She was keen to shift the focus. 'Are you glad you made the move to the city?'

'Well, yes, I can't complain. I live in a suburb

in the foothills of Mount Coot-tha. It's close to the city, so it's a quick commute, but there are plenty of bush walking tracks nearby. I have the best of both worlds really.'

This did sound rather attractive. Despite her love of Paris, Eva had missed the Australian bush. There'd been many times when she'd longed to smell the eucalyptus trees, or to see wattles flowering in winter, bright yellow against a clear blue sky. She'd missed hearing the ridiculous laughter of kookaburras, or catching the occasional sight of loping kangaroos. Tasting the first juicy mango at the very beginning of summer.

They fell silent, but Eva no longer felt quite as awkward as she had earlier. She knew it was foolish to dream, but she almost felt now as if she could spend the entire weekend talking to Griff, getting to know him again.

Not that he would want that, of course.

After a bit, she said, 'It's good that you love where you live. It's important.'

'Yes.' Griff looked at his watch. 'I guess I should make tracks.'

There was almost an hour until the lunch, but Eva supposed he didn't want to hang around chatting with her any longer than was strictly necessary. They'd skipped over the important things, like how they still felt about each other after all this time and why they were both still single. But what could she expect? Her secret had hurt Griff terribly and she was lucky he'd been so tolerant.

Just the same, she couldn't help feeling disappointed that he was so eager to leave.

They rose from their chairs and she showed Griff to the door, where he kissed her on the cheek, a brush of his lips as light as a moth's wings. Such a simple kiss, really, the kind a brother might give, but as Eva felt Griff's touch she caught the scent of his skin and she knew she was as susceptible to this man now as she'd been at eighteen.

She'd felt so adrift this weekend. Torn free from her moorings. And now, without warning, she was longing for the impossible.

She wanted to have Griff's lips on her lips,

warm and seeking. She wanted to kiss him properly, deep and daring, wanted his arms around her as she pressed into his big, powerful body, letting the tight knot of longing inside her unravel and run free.

Griff was so close she was aware of the same tension in him. He made no move to leave and she sensed, in that moment, that they were a hair's breadth from giving in to crazy, nostalgic longing. It would only take one move from Griff and she would be helplessly lost.

Their passion would be stormy, Eva had no doubt, fuelled by years of longing and wondering, of regrets that needed to be assuaged.

A kind of wildness hummed in her veins.

Then she saw it—the warning in Griff's eyes. He wasn't going to make any mistakes this time.

He took a step back.

Not again.

Griff couldn't believe he'd been on the brink of kissing Eva again. Worse. This time, she had been all too aware of how close he'd come.

He could see the knowledge blazing in her eyes. Even more dismaying, he could see that she wanted him too, was almost willing him to kiss her. But that was crazy.

The list of reasons why they shouldn't give in to a kiss was almost as long as from here to Paris. Problem was, Griff couldn't recall a single one of those reasons now. His entire focus was riveted to the woman before him. Eva, the girl who had haunted him for ever. So lovely still.

Pale-skinned, slim as a reed, she was the sweetest temptation he'd ever known. Instead of backing away, he stepped closer.

So close that there could be no turning back.

His hands reached towards hers, just a brush of their fingertips that sent a hot jolt of desire shooting through him. Eva made a soft sound, a catch of her breath, lifted her lovely face to his, let him read the raw want in her eyes, and he was lost.

Their lips met and they kissed hungrily as he backed her into the room, toeing the door closed behind him. This was a storm that had been brewing since they'd first set eyes on each other yesterday and now they kissed with all the fierceness of a passion too long suppressed.

By the time they reached the bed, Griff's shirt had come off, tossed to the floor, and Eva's halter-neck ties were undone.

'We shouldn't,' she said once in a voice urgent with desire.

'I know,' he whispered back. 'This is crazy.'

But, instead of being sensible, they helped each other out of the rest of their clothing, all the while sharing frantic, eager, desperate kisses...

'Is this safe?' he remembered to ask.

Eva nodded, whispered against his lips, 'Yes, I promise.'

He kissed a path from her lovely bare shoulder to the sweet curve of her neck, to her chin. In turn, she nibble-kissed the grainy skin of his jaw while she explored his chest with her hands, possessively sliding her palms over his skin, tracing each dip and plane.

She was breathtakingly beautiful. Her dark silky hair skimmed past her pale shoulders and her slim dancer's body was lithe and supple, her breasts as small and soft and tantalising as ever. As he dipped his head to each needy pink peak, she gave herself up to him with the same wanton eagerness that he remembered from so long ago, and with an emotional honesty that he'd never known since.

It was only afterwards that the guilt came, as they lay together. Eva was on her side, with her back against Griff's broad chest, his arm draped intimately over her hip.

Being with him again had been so exquisitely beautiful she'd come close to the brink of tears again, but she'd been too excited, too stirred to give in to them.

Now, they lay very still, not talking, while their heartbeats slowed, while her mind raced, marvelling at what had just happened.

She'd never dreamed that making love with Griff could be even better than she remembered—so beautiful, so passionate, so breathtakingly intense that it felt as if a spell had been cast over them.

Another blissful memory to hold close.

Sadly, Eva knew that a memory was all this could be—a treasured memory to take with her when she returned to Paris after her surgery. When Griff returned to his busy and important work as a barrister. While they both, separately, tried to forge a new tentative relationship with their daughter. Laine.

Good heavens.

The guilt came with a slam. Why hadn't she been thinking about Laine in the lust-crazed, breathless seconds before they'd finally started kissing each other senseless? Why hadn't Griff remembered her?

A cold shiver shook Eva. How foolish they were, no wiser now than when they'd been eighteen.

And what a cliché—teenage lovers meeting up again years later at a school reunion, unable to resist the temptation of one more fling, for old times' sake.

No doubt they would look back on this as yet another foolish mistake.

Such a pity when, scant moments earlier, she'd felt more joyful than she had in a long, long time. Now she felt almost fearful as she rolled to face Griff.

The intensity in his eyes sent a tremble through her, but he simply stared at her and didn't speak. Time seemed to stretch for ever and they watched each other in silence, almost as if they were afraid to give voice to their individual thoughts, as if they both knew that anything they said now might spoil this perfect moment, might undo the magic. Bring them back to reality, to the admission that this amazing, perfect experience should, almost certainly, not have happened.

But then a faint smile appeared in Griff's eyes and tilted the corners of his mouth. 'Well, that's answered a lot of questions,' he said quietly.

Eva nodded—all the years of wondering were behind them. Now they shared the knowledge that their chemistry was as potent as ever, possibly more so.

He traced the dip of her waist and the rise of her hip with his hand. 'Is this hip painful?'

She grimaced. She'd tried so hard to hide the few moments of pain. 'It catches me sometimes.' Then she couldn't help adding, 'It's one of the problems of an ageing dancer.'

Griff shrugged. 'I guess all dancers have a shelf life, like athletes.'

'I'm afraid so.' Eva almost told him about her planned surgery, but her habit of silence regarding such matters was too deeply ingrained.

Griff stopped stroking her hip and she was intensely conscious of the precise moment he withdrew his hand, leaving her skin suddenly cool where it had been wonderfully warm. He was still watching her closely. 'Do you have a retirement plan, Eva?'

Her heart gave a scared little thump and she sat up quickly. Where was this conversation heading?

'There's no need to panic,' he said. 'I was simply curious.'

Yes, of course. She was overreacting, jumping ahead. His casual question about her career plan was not a signal that he was about to ask her to change her future and to spend it with him.

They'd had sex, nothing more than a nostalgic fling. Eva suspected they were now in a precarious post-coital situation that could be completely ruined by too much talking. And while she and Griff had shared sensational, unforgettable passion, they couldn't really guess at each other's emotions now that it was over. They were still strangers. Really.

They knew each other superficially, but true understanding was impossible after twenty years of living completely separate lives. And now, in this fragile aftermath of lovemaking, it would be so easy to say something stupid.

The wisest move was to allow this day to remain for ever in their memories as an exciting, very moving reunion. A one-off chance to say hello and goodbye before they went back to where they belonged. Apart.

This was closure. Nothing more. Certainly not the start of something new.

Eva just wished she felt happier about letting this go. Why was being sensible always so hard, especially when Griff Fletcher was involved?

Conscious of the growing awkwardness between them, she inched towards the edge of the bed. 'We're going to be late for this lunch.'

'Yeah,' said Griff with a sigh. 'Guess I'd better get going.'

Almost shy now, she wrapped herself again in the towelling dressing gown and she sat on the edge of the bed, keeping her back to Griff as he dressed. She couldn't bear to watch him as he pulled on his clothes. She didn't want to see that powerful masculine body disappear beneath fabric.

Now, she could finally admit to herself that she'd missed this man so much. Too much. And being with him again had confirmed her worst fears—no other man, not even Vasily, could measure up to this—her first love.

After she and Griff parted today, she would miss him all over again. No doubt she would spend the rest of her life missing him. It was such a depressing prospect.

In no time Griff was dressed and standing in the middle of the room, ready to leave. 'I assume I'll see you shortly over at the Golf Club,' he said.

'Yes.' Eva rose from the bed too, and her hip complained. She felt stiff, like an old lady, though she was not yet forty.

She squeezed her facial muscles, forcing her mouth into a grimacing smile. She was sure she should say something about what had happened. But what? 'I suppose I should say thank you,' she suggested.

'Don't you dare. Not that.' Griff looked fierce and it was hard to tell if he was mad at her.

'Anything else feels trite,' she said. 'Or over the top.'

A glimmer of amusement shone in his eyes

and his expression was gentler. For a moment they were kindred spirits.

But I wouldn't dare tell you how I really feel about you, Griff.

He said, 'I should go.'

Eva nodded.

But, instead of leaving, he came around the end of the bed. Cupping her chin, he tilted her face towards him and kissed her again without haste. 'You're the beautiful mother of my child,' he murmured.

Oh, Griff.

Before she could think of an appropriate response, he turned and once again headed for the door.

'See you at the Golf Club,' he said over his shoulder, and this time Eva felt as if she was watching something vital leave her, like her own lifeblood.

CHAPTER FIVE

TIM AND BARNEY had given up waiting for Griff at their prearranged meeting place in the hotel lobby. He showered and changed super-quickly and found them in the bar at the Golf Club. They eyed him suspiciously when he turned up.

'Hello, stranger.' Tim had never been one to beat around the bush.

Griff responded as smoothly as he could and asked them about the reunion golf tournament which they'd both played in that morning. Apparently, his mates had ended up with very ordinary scores and Tim was very keen to change the subject.

'So what's with you and Eva?' he asked in a voice dripping with innuendo.

Griff was used to flipping glib answers in response to almost any sticky question, but he found himself floundering. Truth to tell, he was still coming to terms with everything that had happened between him and Eva.

'We've had a lot to catch up on,' he said, knowing it sounded lame.

Tim rolled his eyes. 'No kidding?'

'Something's come up,' Griff added, because he couldn't fob his mates off indefinitely. 'Something big, actually, and Eva and I needed to discuss it.'

'Hmm.' Tim looked unconvinced.

Barney, who was more sensitive, offered a sympathetic nod. 'Did Eva need legal advice?' he asked.

Griff ignored Tim's scoffing reaction to this innocent question. 'I should be able to fill you guys in soon,' he told them. 'In the car on the way home, perhaps.'

His mates looked intrigued, but at least they stopped needling him, and it wasn't long before they moved on to chat with others. Griff, however, remained, staring into his beer and pondering the crazy turn of events that his life had taken over the past twenty-four hours.

He'd known from the outset that he should have stayed well away from this school reunion. It was supposed to have been a bit of harmless fun with a few mates. *Ha!* The fun had turned serious from the moment he'd set eyes on Eva.

Being with her again had proved even more devastating than he'd feared. She'd thrown him into a total tailspin, which even now didn't really make sense.

What was it about the woman?

Why was his behaviour so out of control?

Sure, Eva had been his first love. So what? Every guy had a first love. Running into her again at a school reunion wasn't supposed to be a big deal. It made no sense that he'd behaved like a lost and lovesick soul responding to some mythical siren's call.

The result? Naturally, he'd crashed headlong into dangerous rocks.

With a heavy sigh, Griff picked up his beer glass and stared at it, and then set it down again without tasting it. Beer was a drink he enjoyed when he was relaxed, but today his thoughts and his stomach were churning.

As a lawyer, he'd had plenty of experience in analysing the behaviour and motives of others, both the innocent and the guilty. Now it totally bugged him that he couldn't understand his own behaviour.

He could hardly plead that he and Eva had been in a motel room, and the whole time the damn bed had been there—just *there*, mere feet away from them—the hugest temptation known to man.

At least Griff was certain of one thing. He knew that he wanted to be a part of Laine's future. And he was damned if he'd keep her a secret. She'd been a secret for far too long.

Strangely, his feelings about Laine were surprisingly clear-cut and straightforward. While his feelings for Eva—

Griff let out another heavy sigh. His feelings for Eva were a different matter entirely, defying reason and logic. Eva was like a drug for him, like pollen to a bee. Irresistible.

More than that, he now realised with a shock, his first girlfriend had remained the yardstick by which he'd measured every woman he'd met since. With the grand result that his love life was a stuffed-up mess.

'Oh, there you are!' Jane Simpson almost pounced on Eva as she arrived at the lunch. 'I was worried that you'd had to leave early and we'd missed saying goodbye.'

'No, still here. Sorry I'm late.' Eva reached into her shoulder bag. 'I found some *Swan Lake* programmes in my suitcase and I've signed them for your daughter and her friends. And Barney's daughter, Sophie, as well. I gather they're all ballet-mad.'

'Oh, Eva!' Jane's eyes were huge with excitement. 'How wonderful. The girls will be ecstatic.'

She studied the programmes Eva offered, looking with particular interest at the photo on the front cover of Eva dressed as Odette in a white tutu and the famous white feathered headdress.

Jane touched the signature scrawled in black ink. 'We'll have this framed. Our little Molly can hang it on her bedroom wall. She'll be so thrilled. All the girls will be. Eva, that's *so* thoughtful. Thank you.'

'Not at all. It's my pleasure.' Eva could see Griff at the far end of the room near the bar and, despite the magnetic pull of his tall, dark-haired, broad-shouldered physique, she was happy to linger with Jane and her circle. After the intensity of her weekend, it was a relief to listen to other people's holiday plans, or to answer their questions about her life overseas, or about her mother, whom many of her school friends remembered fondly.

Which was no surprise. Eva's mum had always come across as relaxed and easy-going, with a great sense of humour. The only subject Lizzie Hennessey had been serious and strict about was Eva's dancing and that hadn't happened until Eva was into her teens, when people in the know started to comment on her daughter's rather special talent.

To everyone else in Emerald Bay, Eva's mum, in her tie-dyed hippie sarongs and silver ankle bracelets, had always seemed laid-back, almost to the point of carelessness. Only Eva and her ballet teacher had seen Lizzie Hennessey's super-focused, competitive edge.

Eva was about to take her place at one of the long tables set for lunch when she noticed Laine moving among the guests with a drinks tray. It was hard to keep her eyes away from her daughter. Eva wanted to watch her every move, every smile. Was it her imagination, or did the girl look pale and tired?

Excusing herself, she made her way over to her. She took a deep breath. 'Hi, Laine.'

Laine turned to her and her smile brightened at once. 'Eva, hi.'

'I just wanted to catch you, in case you got too busy later. I'm sorry we haven't had more time to talk. It was such a shock to meet you last night.'

'Yes, I know.' The girl smiled, but her eyes were a little too shiny.

'I wanted to make sure I thanked you for coming here to the Bay, for finding me—finding both of us.' Eva took a quick calming breath. She was in danger of becoming too emotional again.

She handed Laine a piece of paper with her carefully written contact details. 'I'll be in Brisbane in a week or so.'

The girl's eyes widened. 'So we can meet up again? That'd be awesome. Griff and I are planning to catch up for coffee.'

'Oh?' So Griff had already spoken to their daughter. This was wonderful news, of course, a perfect outcome from an imperfect situation.

After Eva returned to Paris, Griff and Laine might continue to see each other regularly. Eva was dismayed by the ripple of envy this possibility caused.

'That's lovely,' she said. 'I really hope you can stay in contact with Griff.'

'Yes, he's rather cool, isn't he?'

The girl didn't know the half of it.

'Where's Laine?' a bossy woman's voice called sternly.

'I've got to get back to work.' Laine made a throat-cutting gesture with her finger.

The contact was far too brief.

'Please call me,' Eva called after her as she hurried away.

'Yes, of course,' Laine called back.

Eva's eyes were so misty she could barely see.

It wasn't till the end of the lunch that Eva spoke to Griff. The final speeches had been made and plans for an Emerald Bay High School Facebook page were launched, along with mention of another reunion in ten years' time.

Eva supposed everyone was wondering, as she was, where they might be or what they might be doing in another ten years. She certainly had no idea about her own future, although she was pretty sure she wouldn't still be dancing.

She wondered about Griff's plans. Would he become a judge like his older sister? And what about Laine? What would she be doing in another decade? This question brought an unex-pected wave of desolation.

'Eva.'

She jumped when she heard Griff's voice close behind her. She turned quickly and wished her heart wouldn't leap at the mere sight of him.

'The boys and I will be heading off soon,' he said.

'Yes.' She rose from her chair. 'You're driving?'

'Yes, with Tim and Barney. What about you?'

'I'm flying back to Brisbane, then I have an-other flight up to Cairns first thing in the morning.'

He nodded. 'To spend time with your mother.'

'And her husband, yes.' Eva hated that their conversation was so stiff and careful, so differ-ent from their earlier steamy passion.

She had to forget that passion now. She had no rights to Griff. She'd given those away many years ago.

'And then I guess you'll be heading back to Paris?' he asked.

'More or less.' Again, Eva chose not to tell him about her surgery. The operation and the weeks of physiotherapy that would follow were ordeals she planned to endure in private.

It wasn't merely a matter of pride. The fewer people who knew about her condition, the fewer chances there were of word getting out and filtering back to her ballet company, damaging her career prospects.

Griff drew a deep breath that expanded his chest and made his shoulders seem wider than ever. 'It's been good to see you again, Eva.'

'You too.' She tried for a smile, but couldn't quite manage one. It didn't help that Griff looked as tense as she felt, and it certainly didn't help that her mind kept flashing to memories of him touching her, teasing her, bringing her to ecstasy.

'I'll try to keep an eye on Laine,' he said.

'Yes, she told me you were going to meet for coffee. That's great. I…I'm really pleased.'

Griff nodded and the muscles in his throat rippled as he swallowed.

It was tempting to believe, in this moment,

that he cared, that he might even be keen to be a part of her future, but Eva knew this wasn't realistic. She shouldn't allow herself to be distracted by foolish whims. She had to remember the clear goals she'd set herself before she'd set out for this reunion.

A quick catch-up with her old school friends was to be followed by her surgery, and then her return to Paris.

She was going back to her lovely apartment, to her home. To the city she adored, to the career she cherished.

Her only focus now was to beat this hip problem, to remain dancing for as long as she could.

'I guess it's goodbye, then,' Griff said.

Goodbye. It shouldn't matter that it sounded so final but, for Eva, leaving Emerald Bay today suddenly felt as difficult as it had been twenty years ago, when she'd driven off with her mother and had wept all the way to Bowen.

Griff kissed her cheek and she suppressed a choked gasp, which could so easily have turned into a sob.

Be strong, Eva. Don't you dare make a scene.

'Goodbye, Griff,' she said, returning his kiss, and somehow she dredged up the semblance of a smile.

He gripped her hand hard and she saw the look in his eyes that she remembered from all those years ago, the look that told of a deep and powerful emotion. Just as it had in the past, the look reached deep inside her, wrenching at her heartstrings.

Now, as he stepped away, she had to open her eyes very wide to hold back the welling tears. Then he began to walk towards the door where his friends were, no doubt, waiting.

'Griff!' she called, his name springing from her lips instinctively.

When he turned to her, his eyes were once again cautious. 'Yes?'

'Can I just ask one question?'

'What is it?'

Eva took two steps closer. 'You never ever came to watch me dance, did you? Not to any of the concerts?'

A muscle twitched in his jaw. 'No, I'm afraid I didn't.'

Of course it shouldn't have still bothered her after all this time, but she couldn't help pushing for an answer. It was like picking at the scab of an itchy sore. 'Can you tell me why?'

At first he didn't respond, but then he gave a sad, off-kilter smile. 'It was never my world. But I knew you'd light up that stage. I didn't have to see you to know that. You were born to dance. Born to win.'

With that, he continued on his way. His back was straight and his shoulders squared, his head high, and this time he didn't turn back.

'Guess who turned up at the school reunion.'

Eva and her mum were drinking tea on the balcony of the new house in Cairns, which had been built by Lizzie's husband, who had his own building firm. It was a beautiful modern place, constructed of timber and with masses of glass, and set on a rainforest-covered hill with spectacular views of the Coral Sea. So different from the humble two-bedroom cottage that had been Lizzie and Eva's home in Emerald Bay.

Lizzie shrugged. 'How can I guess? I don't suppose your old boyfriend would have gone to a school reunion. He's such a bigwig these days. What's his name again?'

'Oh, Mum, don't pretend you've forgotten. You know it's Griff. Griffin Fletcher.' Even the simple act of saying his name aloud sent a jolt through Eva. 'And Griff *was* there, as a matter of fact, although I don't think it was voluntary on his part. I suspect his mates, Tim and Barney, dragged him there, virtually kicking and screaming. But someone else was there too.'

Her mother frowned. These days she had replaced her hand-dyed sarongs with much more elegant clothes, like the white linen trousers and green silk shirt she was wearing now. Her frizzy and greying ginger hair had been professionally straightened and bleached to a sleek and sophisticated ash-blonde bob, and her toenails and fingernails were carefully painted. But, despite the new glamour, Lizzie looked uncomfortable now, as if she sensed that Eva might be trying to catch her out.

'Well, I can only assume it has to be one of your classmates, Eva. I'm sure Jane Simpson would have been there. But heavens, I can't be expected to remember all their names.'

'Laine was there too,' Eva said quietly.

A fearful light crept into Lizzie's eyes. 'Laine? Not…not your…' She stopped, as if she couldn't bring herself to finish the sentence.

Eva nodded. 'My baby. Your granddaughter.'

Lizzie swore softly, an echo from her rougher past. 'How on earth—?' She swallowed, looked distressed.

'Laine was working there as a waitress, Mum. She'd found out that both Griff and I were going to be there and she managed to score a casual job, just for the weekend.'

Lizzie paled, gave a dazed shake of her head. 'For heaven's sake.' She reached for her teacup but her hand was shaking and she set it down quickly, clattering against the saucer. Eventually, she asked, 'What's she like?'

Eva could well imagine her mum's shock and she gave her as many details as efficiently as she could, explaining about Laine's appearance, her adoptive parents, her law studies.

'How amazing,' Lizzie said when Eva had finished, and she looked much calmer now. 'Well, I guess that's all turned out lovely, hasn't it?'

'In some ways,' Eva agreed.

'In every way, Eva. You were able to have your brilliant career. And I'm sure Laine made the Templetons very happy, and it seems they've looked after her beautifully and sent her to uni and everything. I can't see any downsides.'

'Except for the fact that I've missed her,' Eva said in a voice tightly choked by emotion. 'I've missed my daughter dreadfully, Mum, every day for the past nineteen years.' As she said this, the pain welled inside her again, bringing with it a rising tide of misery. Eva closed her eyes and pressed a hand to her mouth to hold back the threatening sobs.

'Oh, Eva.' There was sympathy in her mother's voice, but exasperation too. 'You can't mean that, darling. Don't exaggerate. You've been so busy with your dancing. It's been such a wonderful and fulfilling career for you.'

'Oh, yes,' Eva said tightly. 'Of course, I've had my dancing.'

And she heard Griff's voice.

You were born to dance. Born to win.

The struggle with her tears was huge, but she was determined not to give in. Not now, in front of her mother. She'd shed enough tears in the past couple of days to last her a lifetime. But, given the pain she felt now, Eva had to wonder why on earth she'd thought it was a good idea to come back to Australia.

If she'd stayed in Paris, she could have kept herself cocooned, safe from the truth. Her loss would have been there like a stone in her heart, but Laine wouldn't have been a visible fact, living and breathing and real. The pain wouldn't have been nearly as intense and unbearable as it was now.

Now, having seen Laine and Griff again, Eva knew exactly what she'd lost and it was hard to believe that she had ever thought that dancing was more important than those two very special human beings.

Even the knowledge that Laine had been well cared for wasn't nearly as comforting as it should have been. It could never undo the fact that Eva had given away her precious baby, and had denied herself the chance to be with Griff, as his lover, as his life partner, as the mother of his child.

'You're not blaming me for this, are you?' Lizzie asked in a soft, almost frightened voice. 'Do you think I forced you to...to give Laine away?'

It would have been so easy to lay the blame at her mum's feet, but Eva couldn't be so cruel. Besides, she knew it wouldn't relieve her pain. Seeing her mother's distress would only make everything worse.

'No,' she said firmly. 'I'm not blaming you, Mum. Ultimately, it was my decision.'

'But I do feel guilty,' Lizzie said.

Eva managed a small smile. 'I'm beginning to

suspect that most mothers manage to find reasons to feel guilty, no matter how hard they try to do the right thing.'

Lizzie watched her for a moment with sorrowful eyes, then she smiled sadly and rose from her seat, arms outstretched. 'Come here,' she said. 'I'm sure a hug always helps.'

As her mum's arms closed around her, Lizzie wished she and Laine had hugged like this. It was true. A hug always helped.

Then she spoilt the moment by wishing she'd received a healing hug of forgiveness from Griff. Their passion had been something else entirely.

CHAPTER SIX

ON THE SECOND day after her surgery, Eva could walk with the help of crutches, and she was returning from the bathroom when she saw a tall masculine figure standing at the end of her bed. Not a white-coated doctor, but Griff in a dark suit and tie. She was so surprised she almost stumbled.

Griff quickly stepped to her aid, cupping her elbow with a steadying hand. 'I didn't mean to startle you,' he said. 'Are you OK?'

'Yes, of course,' she responded a little too abruptly. 'What are you doing here?'

It was only then that she saw how worried he looked.

'I came to ask you the same question. What happened, Eva?'

'It's just my hip,' she reassured him, adding a shrug to show that it was no big deal.

Griff's relief was obvious and Eva wondered what he'd imagined might be wrong with her. The fact that he'd been worried bothered her. He wasn't supposed to care. They were going their separate ways now.

'Can I help you back into bed?' he asked.

Eva had been managing this by herself, but that was without the weak knees that Griff's presence caused. 'Thank you.' Despite the shock of his sudden arrival, combined with the embarrassment of being caught in her nightgown and without any make-up, she was truly grateful for his strong arm around her as she eased onto the bed and then carefully negotiated the new hip into position, bolstered by a pillow.

Nevertheless, she felt compelled to quiz Griff as soon as she was settled with more pillows plumped behind her. 'How on earth did you know I was here?'

'Laine told me.'

'Laine?' This didn't make sense. 'But how did

she know? I certainly didn't tell her.' So far, Eva had only exchanged a few brief text messages with their daughter. She'd been determined to lie low until her hip was properly healed. Now, she couldn't decide whether she was pleased or dismayed to have been caught out. By Griff, of all people.

To make matters more complicated, instead of sitting in the available chair like any normal, polite visitor, Griff had taken off his jacket and tossed it onto the visitor's chair, then loosened his collar and tie and perched on the edge of Eva's bed.

He looked far too sexy. Eva found herself taking far too keen an interest in the way he looked. She couldn't help admiring the strong lines of his clean-shaven jaw, the expensive cloth of his trousers, the crispness of his white shirt and the way his shoulders filled it, almost straining the seams. She supposed he'd come straight to the hospital from court.

'Laine tried to ring you,' he explained. 'But you were just coming out of the anaesthetic. Apparently, the nurse who was with you tried to hand you the phone, but you were too groggy. The nurse was very apologetic, and Laine couldn't get any more out of her after that.'

Griff gave a shrugging smile. 'So then she rang me. We realised you must be in a hospital and we were worried, of course, but I managed to track you down. I happen to know one or two doctors who work at this hospital.'

'You and Laine are becoming quite a team,' she said, hoping she didn't sound too crushed.

'Well, it's early days. But she seems open to having a relationship. And I want that chance, Eva.'

'Yes. Of course.' Eva felt hope bloom. Until now, she hadn't dared to hope that she and Laine might be able to bridge the chasm of years and secrecy. Was it possible? For her and for Griff?

In a few weeks she would return to Paris, but Griff and Laine would continue to see each other. Over the coming months, they could become closer and closer.

She quickly stifled the niggle of jealousy that

this scenario kindled, and she realised that Griff was frowning, eyeing her sternly now.

'So what's the story, Eva?' he asked. 'What's your situation? I assume you've had some kind of surgery?'

'A hip replacement,' she said with an accompanying eye-roll. 'It makes me sound like a granny, doesn't it?'

He gave an awkward smile and shrugged. 'I'm sure that must be painful. How are you feeling?'

Old, stiff and sore. 'Wonderful,' she lied. 'I'm making fabulous progress, so I'm told.'

'That's great. And you're super fit from your dancing, so I'm sure you'll break records when it comes to healing and rehabilitation.'

Well, yes, she needed to break *world* records if she was to return to dancing as a prima ballerina. The thought of the weeks of hard work ahead of her was a daunting one, but she'd been tough in the past and she supposed she could be tough again.

'So how long will you be in hospital?' Griff asked.

'Probably only another day.'

'And what then?'

'I'm moving into an apartment nearby and a nurse and physiotherapist will visit.'

Griff was frowning again. 'It won't be much fun, stuck in an apartment on your own.'

'This isn't about having fun, Griff. It's about recovery. Anyway, I live in an apartment on my own in Paris.'

'That's different.'

Eva dropped her gaze. She was very aware of how gruelling the next couple of weeks would be. And yes, it was true that her life in Paris was very different. In Paris, she spent most of her time at the dance studios or rehearsing or performing. In her spare time she visited her friends, or hung out with them at a variety of fascinating venues. Even when she was on her own, there were galleries, theatres, cafés and gardens all within an easy walking distance.

'I'll be fine, Griff. I plan to get plenty of reading done.' She tilted her chin to a determined angle.

Griff didn't look impressed.

* * *

Eva was putting on a brave front, Griff decided.

He watched her grim little smile, the wariness in her eyes and he was sure she was trying very hard to hide how vulnerable and scared she felt.

After all, she'd put everything she had into her career. She'd given up her child for it, and now she faced the very real danger of losing everything she'd worked so hard to attain.

And now she was going to vanish from his life again, hiding away in some grim apartment until she was well enough to hurry back to Paris, leaving him with a raft of unanswered questions.

Who was Eva Hennessey now? Really? How did she truly feel about Laine? Who were the men in her life? For that matter, how did she feel about him?

At the Bay, their bubbling chemistry had been out of control and it had got in the way of sensible, useful conversation. After they'd made love, they'd both been so careful, so worried about saying the wrong thing.

Griff, however, was a man who liked to have

answers. In his work, he applied himself diligently to understanding his clients, to getting to the truth.

And yet Eva, his first love and the mother of his child, was still an enigma.

'You're very welcome to stay at my house,' he said.

Eva knew she must look shocked. She was. Totally. Shocked. Not only was Griff's proposal a bolt from the blue, it was unwise from every angle.

'I couldn't possibly stay at your place,' she said in a breathless whisper.

To her annoyance, Griff merely smiled. 'Ah, but that's where you're wrong. It would be *very* possible for you to stay there. My house is quite roomy. It's all on one level, so it's easy to get around. It's also fairly central, so it's not too far for a nurse or physiotherapist to travel. And I have an exercise bike and a swimming pool, which I'm sure would be quite useful for your rehabilitation.'

This did sound wonderfully convenient, but Eva was sure spending more time with Griff would be totally unwise. They'd said their goodbyes at Emerald Bay and she'd spent most of her time in Cairns carefully filing her memories of Griff Fletcher back where they belonged. Well and truly behind her. In the past. Yet again.

Or at least she'd been *trying* to file them away, with disappointingly poor success.

'Look,' he said, watching her carefully. 'I know this is awkward, after what happened at the Bay.'

What happened at the Bay...

Such a causal summing up of their lovemaking, which had been for Eva the most passionate and beautiful encounter of her adult life.

Griff's expression was guarded now, and he swallowed as if he might be more nervous than she'd first imagined. Even so, the flash in his eyes set sparks inside her.

'I know jumping into bed wasn't our smartest move,' he said. 'But perhaps it was something that had to happen.'

'I suppose you're talking about closure,' Eva said quietly.

'Something like that, yes.'

An awkward silence fell. Eva made a show of smoothing the bed sheet over her legs.

'The point is,' Griff went on, 'I'm not trying to entice you to my place now for any other reason than friendship.' Without waiting for her response, he rose from the edge of her bed and walked to the window, staring intently out.

She knew there was nothing to interest him out there—nothing more than the other hospital buildings.

'I don't like to think of you holed up in some apartment when my place is available,' he said quietly, still facing the window.

After a bit, he turned back to her and his eyes betrayed the merest hint of a smile. 'I've done my best to reassure you, Eva. You don't need to look so worried.'

It might be simple for him to make this offer but, obviously, he had no idea how susceptible she was. How vulnerable. He didn't understand that being with him again brought everything back. All the old longing and pain and hope and despair.

'It's very kind of you,' she began.

He was waiting for her to continue, to accept or reject his offer, and Eva knew it was time to make her own position crystal-clear.

'I'll be leaving Australia as soon as I can, Griff. I'm going back to Paris. I've set myself a huge goal, you see.'

'That's commendable.'

She shook her head to make her point. 'You asked me if I had a retirement plan, but I don't have one at the moment. I don't want to think about retirement. My goal is to keep dancing for as long as I can.'

'I certainly don't want to stand in your way,' he said firmly. A beat later, he shot her a searching glance. 'But can you really dance at the same professional level that you're used to, after a hip replacement?'

'It's been done.' Eva shoved her chin even more stubbornly forward. 'It's not common, I must admit, but I plan to give it a jolly good try. I certainly won't give up easily.'

'Of course you won't.' This time there was no hint of amusement in Griff's smile. 'And I wouldn't expect anything less from you.' With his back to the window now, he folded his arms over his chest. 'It doesn't change my invitation, Eva. You're welcome to use my house as a staging post.'

'But—'

'Relax, woman. How many times do I have to tell you this isn't a devious plot to try to win you back?'

'No, I know.' Just the same, it was useful to have this point clarified yet again, and Eva hoped Griff couldn't guess the many stupid scenarios her stupid brain had already imagined.

'At my place, you'll almost certainly have more opportunities to see Laine,' he added.

Yes, Eva had already thought of that tempting prospect and, despite her fears, she could feel herself weakening.

Now Griff stepped away from the window and

scooped up his jacket from the chair. Hooking it with two fingers, he slung it casually over one shoulder, a simple gesture that should not have made him look hotter than ever.

'You don't have to give me an answer now,' he said. 'Think about it. I'll give you a call tomorrow.'

'All right.' Eva swallowed. 'And thanks,' she remembered to add quickly, when he was almost out of the door.

'No worries.'

As Griff steered his car back into the heavy lanes of city traffic that streamed past the hospital, he told himself he'd done the right thing by inviting Eva into his home, back into his life.

She was recovering from surgery, after all, so of course they weren't going to be tempted into further indiscretions of the bedroom variety. His invitation truly was, as he'd told her, no more than an offer from an old friend. A friend who needed to lay to rest a few ghosts.

It helped that Eva was as determined as ever to return to her dancing career. It made their ground rules clearer.

Of course they could both handle the proximity without another juvenile meltdown. For God's sake, they were middle-aged people with an adult daughter. It made sense that they should develop a friendly basis for further communication.

The plan was sensible. His motives were rock-solid.

The fact that he'd been scared witless when he'd heard that Eva was in hospital was no longer relevant. She was obviously fine now. He had calmed down and he wouldn't worry like that again.

In fact, a couple of weeks of closer proximity with Eva Hennessey might very well cure him of any lingering lovelorn emotions from his youth. Getting to know her on a purely friendly basis might even clear the way for him to move forward with his personal life. Finally.

A guy could always hope.

* * *

Eva caved in. The decision wasn't easy and she spent a sleepless night. The temptation to spend more time with Griff was both exciting and scary, but the added allure of the chance to get to know Laine was, in the end, too strong. For the past ten days, Eva had thought about her daughter constantly, remembering how she'd looked in her black and white waitress uniform and asking herself so many questions. She was curious about even the tiniest details—even how her daughter might look in clothes of her own choosing.

Did Laine prefer jeans and T-shirts to dresses? Did she like florals or stripes? Was she a fan of solid colours, or didn't she really care? Eva's curiosity about her daughter was voracious, and the next morning, when Griff rang, she accepted his kind invitation.

He picked her up from the hospital that evening in a sleek silver Mercedes with luxuriously soft leather upholstery. He drove expertly through the peak hour traffic, and they arrived at his place, as he'd promised, inside fifteen minutes.

Griff's house was set back from the street behind a tall brick wall painted grey. The house was very modern, with large windows framed in natural timber and concrete walls painted in a slate tone that blended subtly with the garden of native Australian plants. Remote-controlled garage doors slid quietly open, but Griff stopped the car on the driveway and helped Eva out of her seat.

She willed herself not to react every time he touched her. He was only giving her the assistance she needed, after all, but so far her willpower wasn't as effective as she'd hoped. His hand at her elbow or at the small of her back caused ridiculous flashes of heat.

At the front door, she was greeted by a smiling woman with her hair in a tight bun, wearing an old-fashioned apron over her simple blue dress.

'This is Malina,' Griff said. 'She runs my house like a dream and she has everything ready for you.'

Malina was delightfully round, with rosy cheeks and a strong accent that was possibly Polish. While Griff garaged the car, Malina showed Eva to a beautiful spacious bedroom decorated in contemporary tones and with a soft grey fitted carpet. A huge white bed had a rose-pink mohair throw rug folded over the foot and a mountain of pillows in grey and deep pink at its head. A television was positioned for viewing from the bed.

A door led to an en suite bathroom where soaps and lotions and thick fluffy towels were neatly stowed on glass shelving. On the bedroom's opposite wall, a huge picture window looked out onto a hillside covered in bush.

'Ohh...'

Eva stood very still, entranced by the beautiful view of the hillside covered in gum trees with spotted trunks and softly drooping leaves. Every so often, there was the golden glow of wattle flowers and tufts of pale grass stalks sprouted between granite boulders. It was all so distinctly Australian, and so wonderfully quiet and peaceful.

She found it hard to believe that there was a busy road filled with heavy traffic only a block away. Goodness, she could even see a brush turkey, black-feathered with a red and gold frill around its scrawny neck, pecking its way down the hillside on spindly legs.

A wave of nostalgia swept through her and she knew Griff had been right. This was a perfect place for her to rest and to recuperate. And to heal.

'I'll show you the kitchen,' Malina said. 'So you can find the kettle and make yourself a cup of tea or coffee whenever you fancy.'

'Thank you.' Eva followed, walking carefully with the aid of her crutches.

Malina, having left their dinner in the oven, went home and Eva and Griff ate roast lamb and a warm mushroom and spinach salad at one end of the dining table. From here, subtle outdoor lighting showed them a view of the long timber deck that surrounded an elegant swimming pool.

'You have a beautiful home,' Eva told Griff. 'I can see why you love living here.'

He looked pleased. 'I'm glad you like it.'

'I especially love the view of the bushy hillside from my room. I even saw a brush turkey.'

'You'll see plenty of them here. And rock wallabies too.'

'Wallabies!' She smiled. 'Then I'll really know I'm home.'

'Home?' Griff raised a questioning eyebrow.

'In Australia,' Eva quickly clarified.

'So you still think of Australia as home?'

'Well…yes. I…I guess.' It was unsettling to realise that right at this moment her lovely apartment and the glittering Eiffel Tower felt light years away. It was almost as if they were part of another world, a make-believe world, like the props and scenery on the stages where she'd danced.

It was a timely reminder that she had to be super-careful while she was here. She mustn't be seduced by this gorgeous man's kindness, by his lovely home, or by the history they shared. They'd made a pact and it was important to honour it. She had to remember the goals she'd set herself—to return to Paris as strong and supple as ever.

Surely it shouldn't be too hard to remember everything she'd worked so hard to achieve over the past twenty years?

All went well over the next few days. The nurse and the physiotherapist seemed quite happy to visit Eva in Griff's house, and Eva continued to make good, steady progress.

Eva rarely saw Griff in the mornings before he left for work. During the day, Malina was there to provide her with light nourishing meals, and Eva conscientiously went through the gentle exercises she'd been given. Between eating and exercising, she enjoyed reading books from Griff's extensive library.

In the evenings she and Griff had dinner together, and these times became incredibly precious to Eva. She knew she shouldn't look forward so eagerly to their conversations, but she found it fascinating to mesh images of the old Griff she knew from Emerald Bay with the man he'd become.

Primed with a glass of very fine wine, they talked—carefully at first, like old friends who'd been out of touch for twenty years—about the places they'd visited, about music and movies. Griff told Eva about a few of the more fascinating cases he'd been involved with, and she talked about her life in the ballet world. They'd both come across fascinating, eccentric characters and the conversations were often lively and fun.

Eventually they became bolder, even stepping into more dangerous ground by talking about religion and politics and they were surprised to discover how often their views converged.

For many nights they avoided talking about their relationships, but eventually Griff prodded Eva.

'I can't believe you haven't had hordes of men throwing themselves at your feet.'

And so Eva told him about Vasily.

'Eight years?' Griff said, eyeing her with obvious sympathy. 'That's a long time to invest in a relationship that doesn't work out.'

'It is,' she agreed but, remarkably, the pain of losing Vasily seemed to have lost its sting since she'd returned to Australia. Not that she would admit such a thing to this man and he made no further comment.

Their partings each evening were super-careful. No touching, not even a kiss on the cheek. They were sticking to the rules they'd set, but Eva couldn't help noticing that this seemed to be much easier for Griff than it was for her.

Each night when she retired to her room, she spent ridiculous ages thinking about him, replaying in her head everything that he'd said, every gesture, every look. She knew she was falling for him again, even though it was dangerous and stupid.

The days were easier. Each day she felt stronger and could move more easily and she was growing more confident that she really could achieve her goal of returning to the stage.

She just wished she felt happier about that.

CHAPTER SEVEN

IT WAS A few nights later that Griff received a phone call from Laine.

'Can I come round to talk to you and Eva?' she asked. 'It's rather important.'

Excitement and worry duelled inside Griff. He wondered if he should consult with Eva about this, but he was sure she would want this meeting with their daughter. Lately her conversations had often drifted towards Laine. And they were both over the shock now and more than ready to get to know Laine.

'Of course you can come,' he told her. 'But try to make it soon if you can. Eva shouldn't stay up too late.'

'That's nice that you're fussing over her,' Laine said.

'I'm not fussing.' He was being sensible.

Laine actually laughed. ''Course you are.'

Griff suppressed a sigh. 'Just try and keep an eye on the time, that's all I'm saying.'

'I'm on my way.'

He was frowning as he disconnected. He hoped his instincts were right and that he and Eva were more than ready to take this next step.

He found Eva in the lounge room, sitting in an armchair in a pool of lamplight that made her soft, pale skin glow and her dark hair shine like a river of silk. The urge to scoop her up out of that chair and into his arms was as strong as ever.

Damn. He'd thought it would be easier than this.

At least he'd *hoped* it would be easier to have Eva in his home. He'd hoped that after a few days, when he got to know the real, grown-up Eva rather than his romanticised boyhood memory, he would see her imperfections and become a little disenchanted.

Sadly, this wasn't the case.

'That was Laine on the phone,' he told her. 'She wants to come over to talk to us.'

'What did you tell her?' Eva asked quickly. 'You said yes, didn't you?'

'I did.'

'But you're worried? You look upset.'

'Do I?' Hastily, Griff feigned surprise. He was only upset because he still fancied Eva. That wasn't supposed to have happened. 'I'm fine,' he said. 'I think Laine sounded quite excited, actually.'

Eva looked excited now. Her eyes were bright, her cheeks flushed and she got to her feet perhaps a little more eagerly than she should have. 'I've been so hoping for this. Should we offer her some supper?'

'I guess.' Griff held up a hand to slow her down. 'But stay there while I get your crutches.'

'No, I'm OK. I've been walking without them. What would Laine like, do you think?'

Griff watched Eva for a moment, unable to stop himself from staring at her rosy cheeks and shiny blue eyes.

'What?' she said.

Had she any idea how lovely she looked when she was excited?

Her flush deepened under his gaze, but then she looked away, her mouth twisting anxiously. Had she guessed the crazy direction of his thoughts?

'Why don't we check out the freezer?' he replied without answering her question.

'Good idea.' Eva set off purposefully towards the kitchen, 'That Malina of yours is such a gem. She's bound to have just the right thing tucked away in there.'

Eva's heart took off like a rocket when she heard the doorbell ring. Griff went ahead to answer it, and Eva followed as quickly as she could.

Laine was dressed in jeans and a simple paisley print top in shades of lavender and aqua blue. It was the kind of top Eva might have bought for herself if she'd seen it in a shop and she felt a happy-sad pang as she recognised another point of connection to the girl.

Her daughter.

She wondered how she should greet her. A kiss on the cheek? A hug?

No, not yet. She didn't want to rush the poor girl.

'I'm so pleased that you're staying at Griff's place,' Laine said after they'd exchanged polite cheek kisses.

'Yes, it's very kind of him.'

'Kind?' Laine laughed.

Of course Eva was anxious to set the girl straight. 'Laine, you mustn't read anything into this. I'm just staying here while I get over the surgery.'

'Yeah, I know, I know. Griff went to great lengths to explain that you haven't been in touch and have a lot to catch up on.'

But the amusement in the girl's eyes suggested that she still thought there was something deeper going on.

'Yes, well—' Slightly rattled, Eva managed to keep her smile firmly in place as she gestured down the hallway. 'Come in, Laine. Will you have a cuppa?'

They all opted for tea and Griff insisted on looking after this as he didn't want Eva struggling to carry a tea tray, so she found herself in the lounge room with Laine.

Laine seemed quite relaxed, at least on the outside, Eva was pleased to see. While Griff disappeared into the kitchen, Laine asked Eva about her healing hip, and Eva asked her about her studies.

She felt surprisingly calmer when Griff reappeared, handing around mugs and offering the tiny cherry lattice tarts that Eva had instructed him to reheat in the microwave.

Seeing father and daughter together now, Eva noticed similarities between them. The shape of Laine's forehead, the same shade of grey in her darkly lashed eyes, the way she squinted ever so slightly when she smiled.

The girl was sitting with her long legs comfortably crossed. The hem of her jeans rode up a little and Eva could see her shapely ankle and the small butterfly-shaped birthmark she remembered so well.

Stay calm. Remember to breathe.

'These are delicious,' Laine said as she munched on a cherry tart. 'Did you make them, Eva?'

'Um, no.' Eva felt a bit of a fraud, recalling how happy she'd been when she'd found these tarts, as if somehow she'd created them with her own fair hands. In truth, she had very few domestic skills, and she was especially lacking when it came to baking. She'd always been so careful about her diet. 'Griff's housekeeper made them. I just chose them to go with our tea.'

'Well, they're divine.' Laine licked crumbs from her fingers.

'I imagine you have all sorts of questions,' Griff said to Laine.

'Hundreds,' the girl admitted. 'For starters, I was intrigued that you both kept quite separate at that reunion. It was really hard to find the two of you together.'

'That's easy to explain,' said Griff. 'Neither of us knew the other was going to be there.'

'Really?' Laine's eyes widened with obvious

surprise. 'So you didn't communicate beforehand?'

Eva and Griff both shook their heads.

'You mean...you two really haven't been in touch?'

'Not for—' Eva swallowed. 'No, we haven't.'

Laine gave a puzzled shake of her head. 'How long had it been since you'd seen each other?'

Eva avoided making eye contact with Griff, but there was no point in skirting the truth. 'Not since I left the Bay. Twenty years ago.'

'Oh, my God.' Laine's eyes were huge as she took this information in. 'You mean...you only met again at this reunion?'

'Yes.'

Laine turned to Griff. 'So am I right in guessing that you didn't even know about me?'

Eva, sitting in an opposite chair, tensed, clutching her mug of tea.

'No, I didn't,' Griff told her calmly.

Laine swore softly and she no longer looked quite so cheerful. 'So you only found out about me when I burst in on you at the reunion?'

Griff nodded, and Eva realised she was holding her breath.

Laine looked pale as she stared at her father. 'What was it like to find out now, after all this time?'

'A shock, of course.' Griff seemed to be searching for the right things to say, and Eva could imagine him discarding words that were too close to the gut-wrenching devastation that he must have felt on that fateful evening. 'The main thing is,' he said at last, and he even managed to smile, 'I'm very, very happy to know you now.'

Laine nodded, momentarily silenced, but eventually she turned to Eva with clear grey eyes so like Griff's. 'Can I ask why you didn't tell him?'

Whack. It was the question Eva had known must come, but she still wasn't prepared. Where should she start?

In the past she'd excused herself by loading a good share of the blame onto her mother and Griff. This evening she didn't want to lay blame at anyone else's feet. She knew it was time to accept that the final decision had been hers. But how could she justify her choice of a career over mothering her very own baby?

'There were several very good reasons,' Griff said, gallantly intervening on Eva's behalf.

'Well, I really need to hear them,' said Laine. 'I want to know why you made the decisions you made and how you feel about them now. It's very important to me.' Laine looked from one parent to the other, her expression super-serious and intense. 'You see, I'm pregnant.'

Eva wasn't sure whose jaw dropped faster—hers or Griff's. For a moment she could only stare at Laine in shock but, as the truth sank in, she was out of her chair, opening her arms to her daughter. For an awkward moment, she was poised like a bird about to take flight, but then Laine rose too, shyly at first, but at last, with a sob, she launched forward.

'Oh!' she cried as Eva's arms closed around her.

And then they were hugging. Mother and

daughter, weeping and clinging tight. Eva could feel Laine's shoulders shaking, could feel her daughter's warm arms wrapped around her, feel her own love, pouring like a flood.

Twenty years of longing. And now, here was her precious daughter, facing the same potential pain and loss that had caused her so much heartbreak.

They were like this for some time before she remembered Griff. Poor man, standing there beside them, watching on helplessly.

With an effort, Eva released Laine and swiped at her eyes with her hands. 'Gosh, look at us. I think there's a box of tissues here somewhere.'

'I'll get them,' Griff offered, clearly relieved to at last have something to do.

Promptly, he returned from the kitchen with a full box of tissues and Laine and Eva took handfuls and mopped at their faces.

'What a pair we are,' Eva said, managing a small smile.

Laine smiled wanly back at her. They sat down again and picked up their cooling mugs of tea, and Eva wondered if they had woven the first delicate threads in a new but fragile bond. She only wished that the circumstances could have been happier.

Griff retrieved his mug but he remained standing, almost as if he needed to distance himself from their overt feminine displays of emotion. Eva sent him a rueful smile of gratitude and wondered if he was plotting for a quick retreat.

His response was to raise his eyebrows, as if to ask—*where do we go from here?*

It was Laine who spoke first. 'I know it's crazy that I'm pregnant too. Like history repeating itself.'

'For the third time,' said Eva.

Laine frowned at her. 'The third time?'

'My mother was a single mum too. She had me when she was only nineteen.'

Now it was Laine whose jaw dropped. 'Wow.'

Eva offered Laine another shaky smile. 'I'm sorry. I really am sorry for you, Laine. It's a hard place to find yourself, especially hard when you've just started your university studies.'

'Yes,' said Laine. 'Life can be messy, can't it?' She looked at Eva over the rim of her tea mug. 'So, were you adopted too?'

Eva had to take a deep breath before she could answer. 'No,' she said quietly. 'No—my mother raised me on her own—as a single mum.'

Unlike me. Tears threatened again and Eva closed her eyes, drew another deep breath and willed herself not to give in to the urge to weep.

To her surprise, she felt a hand on her shoulder. Griff was standing behind her now and he gave her shoulder a reassuring squeeze. She felt a warm surge of gratitude, but it wasn't helpful to realise after all this time that she might have underestimated this man's capacity for compassion.

'Eva was under a lot of pressure back then,' he said.

'Because of the dancing?' Laine asked.

'Yes,' Griff and Eva answered together. Eva looked up at him and felt a zap of electricity shooting over her skin. It was there again in his eyes—the shimmering look she had never forgotten.

Laine was watching them closely. 'You have an amazing talent, Eva, so I can imagine the pressure.' She set her mug down, folded her arms and crossed her legs. 'I'm not especially talented. I did pretty well at school, but nothing amazing, but I still feel the pressure to just…get rid of this problem.'

Restless, she uncrossed her legs again, sat straighter. 'I haven't told my parents yet—not my adoptive parents at least—or my boyfriend. I'm really struggling with trying to work out what to do. But I'm running out of time. I'm going to have to decide soon. I'd be grateful for any advice. Any words of wisdom.'

Nervously, Eva ran her tongue over her dry lips and she wished she felt wiser. Surely she should have learned some important lessons from her own experiences?

'If you're wondering whether I have regrets about giving you away,' she said, 'I have to tell you that I do.'

Laine nodded, and then she pressed her lips together, as if she was also trying not to cry again. 'But you've had a wonderful career,' she said.

'Yes, I have,' Eva agreed and, until now, she had clung to that career almost as if it were a life raft. But this evening, so far away from Europe, here in Australia with this man and their daughter, she found it hard to remember exactly why her dancing had ever been so all-consuming.

'My parents—the Templetons—are good, ordinary, hard-working people,' said Laine. 'My dad's a teacher and my mum works as an aid in a kindergarten. They've been saving like mad and they're about to go on their first overseas trip. An extended holiday. They're so happy and excited and I'd hate to ruin it by giving them something like this to worry about.'

She sighed. 'As for my boyfriend—he's a med student.' She gave a small uncertain shrug. 'I'm sure he'd be horrified if he had to admit to his circle of very clever friends that he'd slipped up and made his girlfriend pregnant.'

'But you can't be sure that's how he'd react,' said Griff, speaking up for the first time.

Laine frowned up at him. 'I guess—'

'Aren't you planning to tell this fellow?' Griff challenged.

The girl gave a helpless shrug. 'I…I don't know. I'm sure he has no plans to settle down. I'm not sure I want to either. At…at the time, I thought we were madly in love, but we're certainly not…we weren't planning to tie the knot.'

A small silence fell and Eva was aware of the three of them mentally tiptoeing carefully as they negotiated this difficult conversation.

Laine said, 'I was thinking of doing what you did, Eva—having the baby adopted. I mean, I really want to finish my degree, and I can't imagine trying to study and look after a baby on my own, and I don't want to burden my parents just when they're trying to wind down and—'

She looked up, looked directly at Eva, her lovely eyes pleading. 'Was it worth it? Giving me up so you could have your career?'

Eva's heart thumped hard. She'd been terrified of something happening at the reunion, but she'd never dreamed it would end up like this. Now, not only were the secrets from her past exposed but they were being taken out and examined, prodded and questioned. And she had no choice but to face up to the painful truth she'd avoided for so long.

This was no time for cowardice. She had to dig deep, to find the courage to be honest with Laine.

'I can't tell you what to do,' she said, carefully feeling her way forward. 'I have the benefit of hindsight, but you're young and you're facing a very difficult decision.' She swallowed and pushed on. 'It seems to me that difficult choices are hard because there are reasonable arguments on every side. But I think the thing to remember is that giving up a child is not a one-time event. I was told the pain would be temporary, but—'

Eva's mouth pulled out of shape and she had to wait and take a breath before she could go on. 'But it wasn't. The pain's stayed there. And I've relived that day over and over.'

Tears shone in Laine's eyes.

'And,' Eva added without looking Griff's way, 'I feel bad, *really* bad, that I denied a man the right to have a relationship with his own child.'

'I…I see.' Laine looked towards Griff. Her chin trembled and the emotion shining in her eyes spoke volumes.

Eventually, she turned back to Eva. 'But I guess the upside for you is that you're world-famous now.'

Eva shivered. 'That makes me sound so selfish.'

'But it would have been hard to give that up. You must have known when you were young that you had a huge talent. Not many people get to be a prima ballerina.'

'No,' Eva said, but she had to look away, unable to meet the direct grey gaze that reminded her so much of Griff's.

It was difficult to believe that leaving Paris and coming back to Australia could so completely shift her perspective but, right now, none of her choices made the same clear and perfect sense that they always had in the past. Nevertheless, she didn't want to burden Laine with her own crazy confusion.

'I suppose my best advice,' she said carefully, 'is to follow your own heart. Make the choice that's right for you, but also don't jump to conclusions about what other people might be thinking. Griff's right—you should talk to your boyfriend.'

'Right. OK, thanks.' Laine looked at her wristwatch. 'I guess I'd better get going. I promised I wouldn't keep you up too late.'

'I'm fine,' Eva protested, but Laine was already on her feet. 'Thanks for this chance to chat,' she said. 'It's been pretty mind-blowing to meet you guys and I know you can't solve my problems, but it's been really helpful to talk. And…and to get to know you a bit.'

'Well, you know where we are and we're both very keen to stay in touch,' Eva said, also getting to her feet. She tried to smile, but this evening had been so precious. If she wasn't careful, she'd become too emotional again.

Laine must have felt the same way. Having told them that she was leaving, she was backing away fast, but she gave them a teary smile and blew them a kiss as she hurried to the door.

Eva didn't follow as Griff accompanied her. She heard the soft murmur of their voices as they bade each other goodnight and she thought how incredibly fortunate she was that neither Griff nor Laine had been bitter or resentful.

This scene could have been so much uglier.

Letting out a deep breath, she sank into her chair, exhausted. But she was exhilarated too.

She'd met Laine at last. Properly. She now knew exactly what her daughter looked like, how her voice sounded, how she liked her tea.

She looked towards Griff as he returned and lowered himself into a chair opposite her.

'We didn't think to take a photo,' she said.

He rolled his eyes, gave a crooked smile. 'Possibly because there were higher priorities?'

'Yes, of course.'

'And you would have hated the photo, anyway. Your face is all puffy from crying.'

'Yes, I suppose I must look a fright.' Thank heavens she wasn't wearing stage make-up.

They sat for a moment in silence, a surprisingly comfortable silence.

'You did well, Eva,' Griff said gently.

'You think so? Was my advice useful, do you think?'

He nodded. 'It was a tough call.'

'The poor girl. I can't believe it's happening again.' After a bit, she sent him a shy smile. 'Thanks for sticking up for me. You didn't have to. Under the circumstances, it was very good of you.'

'That girl has enough on her plate without having to deal with parents at war with each other.'

'That's very true.' Eva wondered if he had always been this wise. She set down her empty mug. 'I wonder what Laine will decide?'

'I certainly hope she tells her boyfriend.'

'I think she probably will, especially now that she's met you. She was upset to realise how long you—' Eva stopped, and compressed her lips as the weight of her deception brought a fresh wave of despair.

Griff made no comment. After a bit, he said, 'It's getting late.'

'Yes.' There was probably no point in continuing the conversation. Eva knew she would almost certainly get weepy again and Griff had suffered more than his fair share of feminine tears.

But she didn't feel as relaxed as she would have liked. The realities of their past seemed to suck the available air from the room. She was remembering her secrecy, and the way she'd excluded Griff, and then, months later, her painful decision to give Laine away.

As the memories crowded in, she pushed herself out of the chair. She needed to leave before she made a scene. A crushing weight pressed on her chest. Tears stung her throat and eyes.

She couldn't look at Griff, but she felt compelled to speak. 'I'm sorry,' she said tearfully. 'I'm so sorry I didn't give you a chance to be her father.' Then the tears began to fall in earnest.

'Eva.' Griff's voice was rough with emotion.

She felt his hand on her arm, but she shook it away.

'No!' she cried. The very worst thing she could do now would be to fall, weeping into his arms. She was terrified that her willpower would break completely and she'd give in to her overwhelming despair and longing.

She couldn't let this happen. Not after their careful agreement. Blindly, she hurried across the lounge room towards the door to her room, keeping one hand out to steady and guide her past the furniture.

Griff didn't try to follow.

CHAPTER EIGHT

EVA TOOK AGES to get to sleep and, when she did, she dreamed she was back in Emerald Bay...

It was a rainy morning and she was lying in her bed in the little rented cottage where she lived with her mother near the base of the rocky headland. Outside, the waves were crashing on the shore and rainwater was trickling through holes in the guttering. She felt nauseous again. It was the third morning in a row that she'd experienced this queasiness in her stomach. And her period was three weeks late.

Eva knew what these symptoms almost certainly meant.

Her next thought was Griff and then, in the miraculous way that only happens in dreams, she was instantly down on the beach with her surfer boyfriend. The rain had disappeared and it was sunny and his arms were around her. Her cheek was pressed against his lovely tanned and muscly chest. She could feel the warmth of the sun on his skin, could smell the salt of the sea in his rough, dark hair.

His arms tightened around her, holding her closer, and she felt safe and happy and madly in love. Happiness was rising through her like a bright tide of bubbles.

'Don't worry,' Griff whispered close to her ear. 'Don't worry about anything, Damsel.'

Damsel was his nickname for Eva. He'd chosen it after their first dive together on the reef when she'd been so thrilled by the discovery of the pretty little blue and yellow damsel fish.

'But what are we going to do about the baby?' she asked him now.

'We'll become parents,' Griff said, making it sound incredibly simple and OK. 'We'll have a beautiful little damsel of our own and the three of us will live happily and make our lives together.'

'But you have to go to university,' Eva protested.

'Shh.' He pressed a warm finger to her lips. 'Don't worry about that. Don't stress, Eva. I'll find a way to make this work for us.'

Griff was smiling and he looked so certain and confident that she wanted to believe him. But surely it couldn't be that easy? Griff's parents would be furious when they found out about her pregnancy. They might even try to claim that she'd trapped their son.

And yet... Eva could already sense deep inside her that none of this really mattered. A kind of sixth sense told her that Griff would dismiss every one of the problems she raised. No matter what happened, he was going to protect her and look after her and make everything right.

I'll find a way to make this work for us.

'Aren't you even a little bit scared?' she asked.

'No, not at all.'

'Why not?'

He smiled and kissed the tip of her nose. 'Only one reason.' His grey eyes glowed with a deeply stirring emotion. 'You're my Damsel and I love you. I'm crazy about you. And now I get to keep you.'

Eva woke wrapped in a warm cloud of happiness. A peaceful, bone-deep happiness, better than anything she could ever remember.

For a blissful few moments, she lingered in that happy space between dreaming and waking. Then a kookaburra laughed in a tree outside her window. She opened her eyes, saw that she was in the back bedroom in Griff's house in Brisbane and reality came crashing back in all its cruel and harsh bleakness.

Griff had never made such beautiful promises to her. She'd never given him the chance. Instead, she'd kept the pregnancy a dark secret and had taken the long and lonely road on her own to fame and glory.

Now, cold misery swept in to replace the happy warmth. Eva lay stiffly in her bed, listening not to the sea but to the sounds of Griff moving about in the kitchen, making coffee for himself.

Soon she would hear his departing footsteps in the hall and then the front door closing behind him, the car backing out of the garage. Then there would be silence until Malina arrived in about half an hour's time.

This was the pattern of their mornings. It was part of the deal Eva and Griff had settled on when she'd arrived as his house guest. His *temporary* house guest.

Unhappily, Eva threw off the bed covers and started the morning exercises she'd been assigned by the physiotherapist. First, while she was lying down, there were ankle pumps and rotations, knee bends, buttock contractions and leg raises. Then, standing, she did more knee raises, hip abductions and hip extensions. Later she would use Griff's exercise bike.

She was being very conscientious about this regime. Of course she was. Looking after her body was second nature to her.

If only she could shake off the lingering sense of loss. This morning a blanket of sadness enveloped her like a heavy fog that wouldn't lift. She kept thinking about her dream and the words that might have been said but were never voiced, the choices she'd never made.

And now she could only hope that her daughter might have learned an important lesson from her mother's mistakes. She prayed that Laine would make the right decisions and reap the happy rewards.

Two days later, on Malina's afternoon off, Eva was using the exercise bike on the back deck when she heard the doorbell ring.

Her hip was healing well but she still couldn't hurry, so it took some time for her to make her way through the house to the front door.

'Oh!' The caller was a young woman, a very pretty and curvy blonde, dressed to kill in a scoop-necked, tight-fitting black and white polka dot dress and heels higher than anything Eva had ever worn.

The young woman was clearly very surprised to see Eva. Her brightly painted mouth seemed frozen in an O shape as round as her baby blue eyes.

'Can I help you?' Eva asked.

'Is...is Griff home?'

'No. Were you expecting him to be home now?'

'Well, yes, I thought we had an...an arrangement.' The girl pouted.

'I'm sorry, Griff didn't mention that he was expecting you.' Eva was frantically trying *not* to imagine what this arrangement might be. 'I'm pretty sure he's at work.'

'Hmm.' The girl looked Eva up and down rather deliberately.

Dressed in her exercise gear, which amounted to knee-length black tights and a strapless pink and aqua tube top, Eva supposed she must look exceptionally at home in Griff's private domain.

'Who are you?' the girl asked.

'I'm Eva Hennessey.' Eva smiled and offered her hand. 'I'm an old friend of Griff's, a very old friend from way back.'

'Oh, really?' The girl's expression was cautious, her handshake limp.

'And you are?' Eva kept her bright smile carefully in place.

'Josie.'

'Hello, Josie, nice to meet you.'

Josie chose not to respond and she gave no answering smile. She was still pouting and obviously quite put out.

Eva did her best to placate her. 'I'm only staying here because I've had an operation,' she said. 'I had to have a hip replacement, and Griff kindly invited me to stay at his place while I was recovering.'

A doubtful eyebrow lifted.

'It was very kind of him,' Eva hurried on, needing to fill in the gaps in this one-sided conversation. 'But I'm only here for a little while, of course. As soon as I'm fit enough, I'll be flying back to France.'

'France?' Josie brightened at this prospect. Emboldened, she lifted her chin. 'Did Griff tell you about our plans for the weekend?'

'I don't think so.' Eva hoped she hid her surprise, not to mention the ridiculous jealousy that this news aroused.

'He didn't say anything?' Now Josie looked crushed.

'Well, maybe he did mention it and I've forgotten,' Eva quickly amended.

'We're going to Stradbroke Island.'

'How…lovely.'

To Eva's dismay, she found herself noticing all the attractions this woman had to offer—attractions that she lacked. Josie was younger, probably not yet thirty, and meticulously made-up, whereas Eva hardly ever bothered with make-up at home. After so many years of wearing heavy stage make-up, she loved cleansing her skin and using nothing more than a little light moisturiser, but she supposed she must look exceptionally plain by comparison with this pretty creature. And Josie's curving bust line and high heels were attributes Eva could never hope to achieve.

Not that any of this should matter. They didn't matter. Of course they didn't. Eva wasn't trying to win Griff's affection, and his private affairs were none of her business.

Just the same, she couldn't help feeling a teensy bit hurt that he hadn't thought to mention his plans for spending the weekend away.

Josie still looked unhappy and Eva wished she could feel more pity for the girl. She did her best to reassure her. 'As I said, I knew Griff years and years ago when he was still at school. We're just friends. I live in Paris and I'll be gone from here just as soon as I'm strong enough.'

Afterwards, when Josie had driven off in her little red sedan, Eva wondered if she'd overdone the reassurances. Then she wondered if she'd needed the message that she and Griff were not an item even more than Josie had.

It was almost seven in the evening when Griff rang. 'I'm running overtime tonight,' he said. 'There's a complicated case on the go and I need to do more research. You should eat without me.'

Eva knew this was a perfectly reasonable request. 'All right,' she said and she hoped she didn't sound disappointed.

'Or you could meet me in the city for dinner,' Griff amended quickly. 'If you can wait another hour or so, I'll take you to dinner somewhere nice.' He sounded rather pleased by this new idea.

'Malina's made a lasagne,' Eva told him.

'That's OK. We can have it tomorrow, or Malina can stow it in the freezer.'

'I guess.'

'Come on, Eva. You've been stuck in that house night and day. You need a little brightening up.'

Eva couldn't deny she loved the idea of an outing and dinner somewhere *nice*, with Griff as her companion, had very definite appeal. Already, her mind was running through her wardrobe. Would she wear the grey silk dress with the deep V back? Or something more casual?

Then a chill ran through her. 'Will Josie mind if I'm dining out with you?'

'Josie?' Griff repeated sharply.

'The pretty blonde who seems to have a special arrangement with you? And an important weekend planned? On Stradbroke Island?'

'Oh, hell.' He swore softly.

'Surely you can't have forgotten Josie?'

'There was nothing to remember,' he said quickly. 'But don't worry, I'll call her. What about tonight? Will you come to dinner?'

Eva hesitated. Now that she'd had time for second thoughts, dinner in the city felt like a date, and she and Griff weren't supposed to be dating.

'I'll send a car for you,' Griff said.

'But—'

'Damsel, you're not getting into a stew over this, are you?'

She couldn't believe he'd called her Damsel. After all this time. Echoes of her dream whispered through her, bringing ripples of warmth.

'I gave you my word before you moved in,' Griff said. 'You've got to trust me. There won't be any pressure.'

'I know that. I do trust you, Griff.'

'Good. Then you'll come? Don't worry about

getting dressed up. We can go somewhere casual. There's an Italian place near our chambers. You'll love it. They do amazing pasta.'

'All right. I'd love to come. Thank you.'

'Good. I'll send the car. Expect it shortly after eight.'

Griff consulted with his secretary about a missing file and held a phone conversation with one of the key detectives working on the tricky case he was wrestling with, before he turned to the task of ringing Josie.

'Who's Eva Hennessey?' the girl demanded almost as soon as he got through to her.

Griff clenched his teeth. He wasn't in the mood for an argument. He had enough on his plate. Besides, he'd never made any promises to Josie. She was one of those girls who latched onto a casual throwaway line at a party and then made a nuisance of herself. He didn't have time for extra complications right now.

'Eva's an old friend,' he told her. 'From way back.'

'That's what she reckoned too.' Josie sounded petulant.

'Because it's the truth.'

'Yeah? So is that why she gets around your house in tights and a tube top?'

She does? Griff wished he'd been around to witness this. Eva was always very modestly dressed whenever he was home.

'Well, she's a dancer,' he offered as explanation.

'What kind of a dancer?'

A pole dancer, he was tempted to say, but he restrained himself. 'Classical ballet,' he said. Not that it was any of Josie's business. 'Look, Josie, I think you got the wrong end of the stick. I don't think we actually had any plans in place for this weekend.'

'We did. You promised.' She sounded like a little girl.

'No, there was never a promise.' At best it had been a vague suggestion.

'I bought a new bikini.'

Griff pressed two fingers to the knotted frown

between his eyebrows. 'Sorry. I'm extremely busy. I simply don't have time. We'll have to cancel. I've got to go now.'

After he hung up, there was another phone call from Detective Sweeney and Josie was swiftly forgotten.

The Italian restaurant was busy and humming with the voices of happy diners. The place had a rustic feel, with brick archways and stone floors and plain timber tables and chairs, softened by candles in amber glass holders. Tempting aromas of sizzling tomatoes, garlic and herbs hung in the air.

Griff, minus his jacket and tie and with his collar loosened and sleeves rolled back, looked tired but relaxed. And way too sexy for Eva's comfort.

He was waiting at a table and rose to kiss her cheek when she arrived. Eva was wearing white jeans and a simple boat-necked aqua silk top and he smiled his approval, letting his gaze linger on her.

She tried to ignore the flush of pleasure this caused. 'Were you able to get your problems sorted?' she asked.

'Some of them, thanks. The evidence is finally becoming clearer.'

He explained that he'd been working with a detective and a forensic psychologist on a particularly complicated case. Eva had heard on the news that a local woman had been accused of killing her own children, and she wondered if this was the same case but she didn't ask Griff about it. The details were sure to be unbearably sad and tonight he needed to relax.

They ordered red wine and, when it came, it was rich and aromatic, perfect for sipping while they read through the menu at their leisure, mulling over choices and chatting about favourite dishes and memorable meals from their separate pasts.

Eventually, Eva ordered sweet potato ravioli and Griff chose a seafood linguine dish. When the food came, everything was so delicious they ended up sharing. For Eva, the relaxed intimacy was dangerously beguiling.

As they ate, she mentioned a book she'd found in Griff's library—an inspiring autobiography all about being adventurous and not staying stuck in a safe, secure life.

'I guess it's a bit late for me to be reading that message,' she said.

Griff smiled, but there was a watchful light in his eyes. 'It's never too late to encounter new ideas.'

'Well, yes, that's true.'

'And many people would think you already live a very adventurous life, jet-setting about Europe.'

'Not exactly jet-setting. To be honest, I have a pretty gruelling regime.'

'But more exciting than the life of someone like Jane Simpson, who has spent her entire life in the Bay.'

Eva laughed.

'What's so funny?'

'It's just that I was thinking at the reunion

how nice Jane's life must be, living in a quiet place like the Bay, with her little family and the beach close by, almost like being on a permanent holiday.'

Griff's eyes narrowed, taking on a shrewd air, and it was hard to tell what he was thinking. 'You do realise Jane's very envious of everything you've achieved?'

'Maybe it's a case of the grass always being greener somewhere else.'

'Maybe.' He set down his fork and lifted his wine glass. For a moment he studied the ruby liquid, then he raised his gaze to meet Eva's. 'Jane told me you've been very generous with donations to help Katie Jones.'

'Did she?' The sudden change of subject surprised Eva. Katie was a classmate who'd had a terrible surfing accident in her early twenties.

'Well, actually, Jane told me that you'd been helping Katie too,' she said. 'But, honestly, Griff, it was the least I could do for an old school friend, as I'm sure you'd agree. I felt so devastated when I heard about Katie's accident. She was always such an athletic girl, and she was a promising dancer too. It was just awful to hear she'd been paralysed.'

'Did you know she's trying out for the Gliders, the Australian women's wheelchair basketball team?'

'Wow, that's fantastic. I hope she makes it.' After a bit, Eva said, 'Now *that* takes courage.'

Griff nodded. His gaze met hers and held. 'I suppose we all need courage to make the most of our lives.'

At this, Eva's heart gave a strangely dull thud. Had she made the most of her life? Since she'd come back to Australia she'd felt less and less certain about the choices she'd made. And she was still uncertain about the direction her life should take now.

In terms of her career, she'd been very successful but her inner life, her sense of personal satisfaction had been deeply shaken. She no longer felt grounded and certain.

'Do you think it's courage that we need or wisdom, Griff?'

He watched her for the longest time before he answered. 'I guess courage isn't much good on its own.'

'No,' said Eva and of course she was thinking about giving up Laine. At the time, the sacrifice had felt hugely courageous but, since then, she'd questioned the decision over and over.

'I guess courage without wisdom could lead to people making the wrong choices.'

Griff smiled. 'I assume you're referring to people like Napoleon or Hitler.'

Eva couldn't help smiling back at him. Of course she hadn't been thinking of Napoleon or Hitler at all. She'd been obsessing again about her own mistakes.

Perhaps Griff had guessed this and was wisely leading their conversation away from anything too personal. This evening was supposed to be about relaxing, after all.

'Hello, there. Fancy seeing you two!'

The booming voice brought them both turning to see Griff's mate Tim grinning at them like a fool.

Eva heard Griff's soft groan and immediately sensed the tension in him.

'Well, well, well,' said Tim and, if possible, his grin widened.

Eva decided it was her responsibility to set Griff's old friend straight quickly, before any teasing began. It should have been a simple matter to explain about her surgery and recovery but, no matter how carefully she outlined the properness of their situation, Tim kept up his knowing grin.

'It's just great to see how well you guys are getting on,' Tim said with a smirk and he was still grinning as he left them.

Griff and Eva both rolled their eyes as he headed off. They'd done their best. It was annoying that people like Laine and Tim were so smug while jumping to wrong conclusions. Even Malina had started making comments about how pleased she was to see Mr Fletcher looking so happy these days.

'You're good medicine for each other,' Malina had told Eva only this morning.

Considering their particular circumstances, these weren't helpful thoughts to be having at the end of a very pleasant evening out. A careful silence fell as she and Griff left the restaurant. He took her arm, tucking it firmly and safely under his as he guided her towards his parked car. Eva knew there was nothing romantic about the gesture but, unfortunately, that knowledge didn't stop her from enjoying every sweet moment of close contact.

Their careful silence continued as Griff drove home through the busy city streets. Eva supposed he was thinking about the case he was dealing with, which was a pity. For a while there tonight, he seemed to have put it aside, until Tim's smirk spoiled their happy and relaxed mood.

'Thanks for a lovely evening,' she said, hoping to distract him.

'Yeah, it was great,' Griff said.

In the glow of traffic lights she saw the smile he flashed her way. 'You're good company.'

Zap. The small compliment thrilled Eva way more than it should have.

'I must admit,' Griff said as he steered the car up the steep hill towards his street, 'I thought you would have driven me nuts by now.'

This comment certainly brought Eva swiftly back to earth. 'Why? What did you expect?'

His big shoulders lifted in a shrug. 'There was every chance after twenty years that we'd have nothing in common. We could have found ourselves miles apart in taste, interests. Everything.'

They were at the top of the hill now and, as he steered the car around the corner, Griff let out his breath in a small huff. 'OK, maybe what I should have said was I'd been *hoping* that you'd drive me nuts.'

'Really?' Eva asked, now completely confused.

'Not liking you would have made life a hell of a lot easier,' Griff said.

Was this his indirect way of telling her that he still cared about her?

'Did you know you called me Damsel tonight? On the phone?' she couldn't help asking.

'Of course I know.'

He spoke quietly, giving the words significance. When he turned Eva's way, she saw a fierce, impassioned light in his eyes and she felt as if she'd suddenly caught fire. Until this moment, she'd been sure Griff's use of Damsel was a slip that he hadn't even noticed.

Now, as he turned the car into his driveway, she could scarcely breathe. But, before she could get her thoughts properly sorted, Griff was out of the car and opening her door for her. Once again, his hand was at her elbow as he helped her out.

Apart from her murmured thanks, they didn't speak as he steered her to the front door, but her heart kept up a frantic beating and her skin burned with awareness of his touch.

At the door, Griff waited for Eva to go ahead of him and she felt as tense as she had in her teens, wondering if he might act on the chemistry arcing between them. Would he kiss her?

Oh, help! She was hoping that he would. Hoping desperately, in spite of a thousand inner warnings.

The light came on in the hall, spilling over them. She saw Griff, standing perfectly still, watching her. She could sense the tension in him and she was gripped by the deepest kind of longing. She stayed where she was, not wanting to move, hardly daring to breathe.

Griff didn't move either.

Despite their stillness, they were drawing closer, as if pulled by an invisible string, and Eva knew then that it was going to happen.

All it took was a little courage.

Griff whispered, 'Eva,' and he reached for her.

At the same moment a bell-like noise erupted.

Griff cursed. It was his phone. 'I should take this,' he said with grim reluctance, and already he was reaching into his pocket.

Weak-kneed, heart racing, Eva sagged against the wall. In a daze, she heard Griff's end of the phone conversation. Mostly, it involved him trying to calm someone down.

His face was grave as he disconnected. 'My

client's in a bad way,' he said. 'She's in danger of harming herself. I have to go.'

Eva nodded. 'Of course.'

She was shaken and Griff looked as upset as she felt. They'd come so close, within a hair's breadth, of breaking their careful rules. Wisdom had flown out of the window.

Now, common sense and necessity prevailed.

Griff sighed, however. 'I'll say goodnight. I don't know when I'll be back.'

Eva nodded. 'I'll see you whenever. Good luck—with everything.'

'Thanks.' He managed a quarter smile before he turned and left.

Watching the door close behind him, Eva hoped all would be well with his client, but she couldn't help feeling sorry for Griff too. He'd already put in a long day and heaven knew how much sleep he would get tonight before he faced another busy day in the morning.

She also felt sorry for herself. An important and precious moment had been lost, perhaps for ever. A fragile bridge was still broken.

CHAPTER NINE

GRIFF WAS BUSIER than ever in the weeks that followed. On several nights he didn't make it home till very late, but there were no more occasions when he asked Eva to join him in the city for dinner.

She supposed he'd realised his mistake and, after a great deal of self-talk, she'd accepted that this was for the best. She should be grateful that his work got in the way.

After their indiscretion at Emerald Bay, they knew it would have been beyond foolish to break the careful protocols they'd both agreed on. Grown adults in their late thirties knew better than to give in to the same lusty longings that had led them into trouble in their youth.

On the evenings that Griff was home, they continued with sensible, pleasant conversation over dinner. At times they laughed over funny memories they shared, at others their conversations went deeper, touching on philosophy and politics and current events. But they scrupulously avoided another lapse. Any kind of intimacy was strictly off the agenda.

In the meantime, Eva continued diligently with her exercise regime, and she was becoming so strong and supple that she'd started to believe she might actually return to the demanding dancing roles that had made her famous. Undoubtedly, there were more months of practice ahead of her, but she was used to working hard towards a challenging goal.

Goals always made her life clearer and more straightforward. And, as far as she could tell, Griff seemed to have the same outlook, his own goals being centred around the people he defended in court.

Their clear goals had led them down very different paths, however, and the only true bond between them now was their daughter. Eva supposed she should be grateful that the lines of communication with Griff and Laine were open and amicable for her. Really, that was all she could hope for after twenty years of silence.

Her role in both Griff's and Laine's futures would be minimal. She just wished she didn't have to remind herself of this over and over.

It was during the final days before Eva was due to head back to Paris that Malina called her to the phone.

'Hi, it's Laine,' said an excited voice.

'Hello!' Eva was equally excited to hear from her. 'How are you?'

'Very relieved and happy. I've told my boyfriend, Dylan, about the baby.'

'Well done. And how did he take the news?'

'He was adorable.' Laine sounded over-the-top excited now and her story came tumbling out… Dylan had told Laine that he was madly in love with her and, no matter what, he was determined to find a way to support her. Or, rather, Laine amended, they would find a way to support each other and the baby while they finished their university studies.

They weren't announcing a formal engagement and they certainly weren't wasting precious money on a ring at this point. That could come later, down the track.

'For us it's the baby first and then Dylan's exams, and the wedding much later.'

Eva realised that by that time she planned to be back on the stage in Paris, resuming her career, but she didn't mention this now, while Laine explained her hope to take a semester off, or even a whole year if she needed to, before resuming her studies. Dylan would find a part-time job and he would apply for scholarships, or get an extension on his student loan. He was confident they'd work something out.

'That's—' Eva had to swallow the painful lump that had suddenly ballooned in her throat. Just thinking about her daughter's wedding made her feel tearful and emotional. 'That's wonderful, Laine. I'm so happy for you. Thanks for letting me know. I'll pass the good news on to Griff.'

* * *

Later on the same day she was called to the phone again. This time the call was from a board member of Ballet Pacifique, a prestigious company based in Brisbane.

'Our artistic director is leaving for a job in the Czech Republic in six months' time,' the caller told Eva. 'We're going to need a replacement and our first thought was you, Eva, so we wanted to get in early. I know you have a wealth of wonderful experience in both contemporary and classical dance and we heard you were back in Queensland. I don't suppose we could entice you to stay?'

Eva was stunned. 'How did you find me?' she blurted.

'Oh, the gossip chain in ballet circles is still as effective as ever.'

Eva supposed this rep from Ballet Pacifique also knew about her surgery. The woman probably assumed Eva would never dance again.

'Eva, would you consider an artistic directorship?' she asked. 'We'd love to show you what we do.'

'I've seen your dancers.' Eva had taken herself to see several shows on the nights when Griff was extra busy. She'd been to the symphony orchestra, the Queensland Ballet, as well as the Ballet Pacifique. 'Your dancers are wonderful. I loved their work.'

'Thank you.' The woman sounded delighted. 'That's high praise coming from you. Our company is going from strength to strength and we could offer you quite a generous package.'

Standing there, gripping the phone, Eva was, for a giddy moment, very tempted. An artistic directorship was an obvious progression for a dancer facing the potential end of her stage career. Finding such a position right here in Brisbane was a very alluring prospect, especially as it meant that she would also be able to see Laine and her baby. And she would be only a short plane flight away from her mother. In time, she could introduce Laine to her grandmother.

But—

Of course there were buts.

First, there was Eva's important goal to prove that she could get back to full dancing strength. For weeks now, she'd been working really hard, all the while focusing on her triumphant return to the Parisian theatres.

Then there was the Griff factor.

If she remained in Brisbane, she would stay within Griff Fletcher's radius, but forever keeping at a carefully polite distance.

This shouldn't have been a problem, of course, but, unfortunately, for Eva, it felt like a huge problem. Despite her best efforts to resist the man, she'd fallen hard. Again.

The daily contact with Griff had proved every bit as dangerous as she'd feared it would be. She knew now that she loved him, loved everything about him—the way he looked, the way he thought, the lovely home he'd chosen, the way he balanced his work with his home life. She adored just *being* with Griff.

Problem was—since the night they'd gone out to dinner and had come so close to making another mistake, Griff had backed right away. It was clear that he wasn't prepared to risk starting a relationship with Eva. And she understood that.

She'd hurt him terribly when they were young and she didn't deserve another chance at love with this man. But, given the strength of her feelings, she also knew it would break her heart to live in the same city as Griff when they had no future.

It would be torture to see him at Laine's place while keeping up the pretence of distanced, polite friendship.

Behaving as if she didn't care about him was too hard. Eva knew she couldn't keep up the pretence indefinitely. Her only chance for personal happiness was to escape, to flee once again to the other side of the world.

She was pleased Ballet Pacifique's board member couldn't see her face as she declined the wonderful offer. 'I'm sorry,' she said. 'I'm planning to go back to Paris very soon.'

'Oh, well, that's—I guess—' The woman

sounded truly surprised and disappointed. 'That's wonderful for you, Eva, but it's jolly bad luck for us.'

After Eva hung up, she went for a long walk and forced herself to think about Paris and her lovely apartment and all the people and places she was looking forward to seeing again. Nanette, the concierge of her apartment block. Celeste, who had the flower stall on the corner. Louis, the waiter at her favourite café, all her dancer friends.

Eva recalled her favourite sights. The view of roofs and chimney pots from her apartment, the beautiful gardens nearby, the market stalls, the cathedrals and her own personal landmark, the Eiffel Tower. Surely, if she told herself often enough that Paris was where she belonged, she would eventually remember that it was true.

When Griff came home, Eva gave him Laine's news and of course he was delighted.

'Dylan's from a big family and family is very

important to him,' she recounted, delivering Laine's message as accurately as she could.

She added that Dylan wanted their baby to be part of that 'big happy mob' as he called it. Better still, in his family there were oodles of arms willing to help with minding the baby, so Laine and Dylan wouldn't have to pay too much for childcare.

As far as Dylan was concerned, the most important things were that Laine and the baby remained well and that the three of them were able to be together.

As she shared this with Griff, there was something in his expression—a sadness that made her feel a zap of connection with him. Or was it the sting of her own guilt?

Eva was sure that he was remembering, as she was, that he'd never been given the chance to step up to the role of heroic boyfriend and provider in the same commendable way that Laine's Dylan was doing now.

Laine had gone on and on, adding more and more details to the happy scenario, but Eva didn't pass all of this on to Griff. She was thrilled for her daughter, of course she was. It was fabulous to know that Laine would not be a third generation single mother, and that she would keep her baby and have the backup of a supportive family network.

And it meant that Eva would have no reason to worry about Laine or the little one when she returned to the other side of the world and pushed on with her career dreams. She just wished—

No, she mustn't wish.

She'd made her decision and it would be foolish to change her plans now, especially when it seemed that she wouldn't really be needed even if she stayed here in Brisbane.

To Eva's surprise, Griff took her out to dinner again on the night before she left for France.

This time they went to a seafood restaurant with a wall of glass that housed an astonishing floor-to-ceiling aquarium filled with gorgeous tropical fish. There were striped fish, spotted fish, pink and purple and green fish and, of course, the cute blue damsels with their bright yellow fins.

'I thought you might enjoy them,' Griff said.

'For old times' sake?' Eva asked in a choked voice.

His eyes shimmered in the candlelight. 'At least we have happy memories of the sea.'

'Yes, we do,' she whispered, and she hated that most of their other memories were unhappy.

Even these recent weeks of recuperation, which had been lovely, had been overshadowed by the knowledge that she and Griff could never act on their ever-present sizzling tension. There'd been several times when Eva had wished with all her heart that she hadn't set herself the goal of returning to the stage.

Perhaps, if Griff had asked her to stay, she would have happily changed her mind, but he'd stuck to his word. He'd remained the perfect host and a wonderfully interesting conversationalist and friend, a gorgeous temptation who remained just out of reach.

It was painfully clear that he'd made one huge

mistake in that motel in Emerald Bay and he wasn't going to repeat it.

The hardest ordeal came the next morning when Eva flew back to France.

Griff insisted on driving her to the airport. 'I've kept my diary free,' he said curtly when she tried to protest.

At the airport, he also insisted on helping Eva with her luggage and escorting her through Security, continuing all the way to the queue at the Customs gates, where he could go no further.

During all of this, Eva wondered—or, rather, she *hoped*—that Griff was accompanying her because he had something significant to say to her before she left Australia.

She didn't really think there was a last chance possibility for them, but she wondered if he would express regret that she had to leave.

She wasn't sure what she might say or do if Griff gave the slightest hint that he still held deeper feelings for her. There was a very good chance she would hurl herself into his arms and tell him this was where she belonged, where she wanted to stay. For ever.

Eva's heart fluttered dangerously and her legs felt hollow as she stopped near Customs, a mere metre from the end of the queue. Nervously, she rearranged the straps of her bag over her shoulder. She looked down at her boarding pass and passport, then lifted her gaze to meet Griff's and a painful jolt shuddered through her.

Oh, Griff. The look in his eyes almost felled her. Such sadness, as if he hated saying goodbye even more than she hated to leave.

'So this is it,' he said, giving a sadly crooked smile.

Eva swallowed. 'Yes. Thanks so much for everything, Griff.' Her lips were trembling, but she forced herself to continue. 'You've been very generous—not only with your wonderful hospitality, but in the way you've accepted Laine and…and you haven't tried to lay blame. You were entitled to be terribly angry, but you've been perfect.'

'You make me sound like a saint.' Griff gave a smiling shake of his head. 'Haloes don't suit me.'

A dangerous light entered his eyes, hinting at extremely unsaintly thoughts, and reminding Eva of his kisses, of his touch, of his gloriously sexy lovemaking. She felt a tug of longing deep inside and she almost launched forward, hurling herself against him.

'All the best with the hip,' he said. 'I'm sure you'll make a brilliant comeback.'

Eva choked back a foolish whimper. It was stupid to be upset. Of course Griff couldn't read her mind, and he was behaving exactly as he'd promised. He would do nothing to interfere with her plans of returning to the stage and it was too late for her to suddenly change her goals at the very last minute.

Only the lowest kind of former girlfriend would try to wriggle back into a man's life at the last gasp, when she'd spent weeks being adamant that it wasn't what she wanted.

'Thank you,' she said.

The queue was moving through Customs. Another group of travellers arrived, all happy and excited.

Griff smiled at Eva. 'Give my regards to Paris.'

She nodded. 'Yes, I'll do that.' Despite her breaking heart, she pinned on a bright smile of her own. 'Don't forget to send photos of the baby when it arrives. Laine will probably be too busy.'

'Of course.'

'And I hope you'll see Laine from time to time.'

'I will, certainly. We're going to meet for coffee on Saturday mornings. Actually,' he added with a smile, 'Laine will have peppermint tea.'

'So you'll meet *every* Saturday morning?' Eva couldn't help asking.

'Yes, Laine has a favourite café in Paddington, not very far from my place.'

'How lovely. That's wonderful.' Eva was proud that she said this without giving way to tears, but she'd never felt more isolated and left out.

This was right, though, she had to accept sadly. Griff wasn't burdened by a history of mistakes in the same way that she was and he had slipped very naturally and calmly into his role as a father. For Eva, however, having failed Laine as a baby, she feared she would never feel truly confident about offering her daughter ongoing advice.

Bravely now, she straightened her shoulders. There was no point in prolonging the dreadful agony. She should let the poor man go. 'OK,' she said more definitely. 'I guess—'

'You should go,' Griff supplied.

'Yes.'

She was trembling all over now, wondering if Griff would hug her and kiss her properly in an emotional and passionate airport farewell. He stepped forward, lightly touched her shoulder as he leaned closer.

He kissed her cheek.

'Take care, Eva.'

'You too,' she said, but suddenly she couldn't see him. Her eyes were too filled with tears.

Blinking hard, she cleared the tears and saw his look of agonised despair. The pain was only there in his face for a heartbeat and then it was gone. A beat later he turned and began to walk away from her.

Every cell in Eva screamed for her to chase after him, to tell him they were making a terrible mistake. They belonged together, not hemispheres apart.

But she had no right. She'd given up that right twenty years ago.

Now she had no choice but to join the queue of happy travellers bound for Paris. Within no time, her passport and boarding pass were verified and she was entering the departure lounge. Meanwhile, Griff would be finding his car in the enormous car park and driving back into the city, to his work, to his life, to girls like Josie.

Eva found a seat in a café and ordered a coffee, which sat in front of her untouched, growing cold. She was remembering Griff's words from their farewell at the school reunion.

You were born to dance.

So…it was over. Done. Eva was gone.

As Griff steered his vehicle into the busy

stream of morning traffic, he told himself he was OK. Of course he was OK. He was an old hand at farewelling the women in his life. He'd made an art form out of breaking up with them. And he'd been planning this particular break-up for weeks.

Now, his prime reaction was relief. It was the only sensible reaction.

Griff planned to put the experience of having Eva Hennessey as his house guest well and truly behind him. He'd been crazy to offer his home to her in the first place and the self-control that living with her required had damn near killed him.

He'd got through it unscathed, however. There had been no more mistakes in the bedroom and Eva was safely winging her way back to France, where she planned to stage a magnificent comeback.

Now Griff could look forward to arriving home at the end of a long day, knowing that she wouldn't be there to tempt him with her lithe, supple elegance. Never again would he be driven crazy by the flash of her slim, shapely legs as she curled comfortably in an armchair. He wouldn't be trapped by her bewitching smile, by her surprisingly engaging conversation.

Now he would be able to breathe again, without catching the fresh berry scent of her perfume.

Eva was gone and Griff was relieved. Or at least he tried to tell himself that he was pleased and relieved to wave her goodbye. But, as he steered his car into its customary space in an underground car park, he caught his reflection in the rear-vision mirror.

He saw the bleakness in his eyes, the deep creases bracketing his downturned mouth. He saw an expression of gut-churning hopelessness and he knew the ruse wasn't working.

He missed Eva. Already. *Damn it, he missed her like crazy.*

After all this time, he still wanted her. He was as madly in love with her now as he had been at eighteen. He wanted her in his bed. Hell, yeah. But, more than that, he wanted her in his life.

So many times over the past weeks he'd come close to declaring his feelings, to letting his emotions spill. The only thing that had stopped him was his damned pride.

Put simply, he wasn't prepared to cop another rejection.

He'd accepted Eva's reasons for her initial disappearance all those years ago, and he'd come to terms with her silence about his daughter. But a man could only take so many risks with his heart and Griff Fletcher had learned the hard way that with Eva he could never win. Dancing would always come first.

Now, sure enough, she was heading for Paris, and he had no choice but to bury the pain and move on.

CHAPTER TEN

ONCE AGAIN EVA HENNESSEY'S photograph was displayed on posters all over Paris. The press had caught wind of her five-month break from dancing and rumours had been flying thick and fast about the cause. Now, with the announcement of a new performance, ballet circles were buzzing about Eva's return to the stage to dance the role that had made her famous in *Romeo and Juliet*.

Eva was excited too. Her painful hip was now a thing of the past and the doctors were really pleased with her recovery and rehabilitation. Within the dance company, the choreographer, the director and Eva's primary dance partner, Guillaume Belair, had all feared some sort of imbalance or caution in her movements, but now they declared that her dancing was as fluid and beautiful as ever.

At the end of the dress rehearsal of *Romeo and Juliet* the ballet company had applauded her.

'Dazzling!' the choreographer told Eva as he embraced her and kissed her on both cheeks.

A reviewer, who'd been allowed into the rehearsal, reported in the morning papers that Eva's return was a 'triumph of strength and perseverance' and that she now brought 'a new, more sorrowful edge' to the role of Juliet.

At home in her apartment, Eva felt calm as she went through her customary routine of pre-performance preparations. She had already prepared three pairs of pointe shoes, all of which were likely to be used on the opening night. She always measured and sewed the elastic and ribbons on the shoes herself, making sure they were in exactly the right places. Then she banged the points on a wooden floor to soften them, so that they didn't make a loud, distracting noise when she ran onto the stage.

Getting these details exactly right was vitally

important. Shoes were the basis of everything a dancer did on stage and if her shoes didn't feel right it was like trying to dance with someone else's legs.

There had been a couple of tricky moments, as Eva worked on her shoes, when she'd thought of Laine and her baby that would soon be born, and remembered that tiny baby foot kicking free from the blanket all those years ago. As always, thoughts of Laine were accompanied by painful memories of Griff.

Griff at Emerald Bay, making love to her with heart-wrenching passion. Griff in his home in Brisbane, in the role of charming host. Griff at the Italian restaurant, and their conversation about wisdom and courage.

So many, many times since she'd left Emerald Bay, Eva had been overwhelmed with loneliness and longing. Often she'd come close to picking up the phone to enquire if Ballet Pacifique's directorship had been filled. But then, each time, she remembered Griff's careful withdrawal from her and the pointlessness of going back when all he was prepared to offer her was polite and distanced friendliness.

She was far better off here, pursuing her career.

So today, when her thoughts edged dangerously towards Griff, Eva quickly snatched her mind back from that distracting direction. Dance was an art form that required total concentration on the present. Every movement, every expression had to be sensitive and precise.

She couldn't possibly dance at her best if she was dwelling on the past. And now the day of her comeback had arrived and she had to stay completely focused.

After limbering and stretching, Eva ate a light, healthy breakfast and she refused to allow herself a single thought about Australia. She was Eva Hennessey, about to make a magnificent return, and tonight's performance had to be perfect.

Once this evening's presentation was behind her, she could look forward to many more years of dancing. She had overcome a huge obstacle and was set to continue with her dream.

When the plane touched down at Charles de Gaulle Airport, Griff was surprised by how composed he felt. He supposed it was the calmness that came after finally reaching a decision and then following it up with action.

He was here in Paris to watch Eva dance. For the first time ever, he would sit in the audience and watch her on stage, as she gave all of her heart and passion to the art form she'd chosen over him.

Griff hadn't told Eva he was doing this. They'd had minimal contact since she'd returned to Paris and most of his news about Eva had come via Laine. Griff had scoured the Internet, however, watching for news from Paris, and as soon as stories about Eva's return to the stage appeared he'd been gripped by a strangely forceful desire to see her perform. He now knew that he had to have Eva in his life. He needed her desperately. But he'd also realised that he had no right to her when he'd never bothered to truly understand her passion for dance. At the reunion she'd asked him an important question.

You never ever came to watch me dance, did you? Not to any of the concerts?

At the time, he'd brushed her off. It had taken weeks for the crazy truth to dawn on him, that he'd never been to watch her dance because he was jealous. Jealous of her dancing, as if it were a lover she'd chosen over him.

It was perhaps forgivable from a teenager, but these days Griff was supposed to be older and wiser. And yet he'd continued to cling stubbornly to his crazy prejudices.

Now, at last, Griff knew the time had come to finally face up to his stupidity. His plan was to watch Eva dance and, he hoped, to understand at last what he was up against.

So, yeah, here he was. In Paris, the city of lovers.

After tonight, Griff hoped to be armed with a sufficient depth of understanding to finally win Eva. This time she wouldn't have to choose. He'd make that crystal-clear.

At twelve there was a full warm-up class at the theatre. The dancers, dressed in tights, leg warmers and tops, began, as always, with the very basic positions and steps they'd first learned when they'd begun dancing classes as children.

Eva never tired of going through these simple routine moves that were as familiar to her as breathing and yet so critical to any dancer's technique. She found something very comforting about the sameness of the movements, and the eternal drive to perfect them, while Colette, their rehearsal director, called all the usual instructions.

'Keep the legs turned out.'

'Stretch back, back, back, and now extend to the front.'

Eva knew that these warm-ups were important, not only for preparing her body but also for releasing endorphins to help her feel happy and calm.

Happy and calm, she mentally chanted as she dipped in a *demi plié. Happy and calm,* she thought again, keeping in time with the beat from the piano as they moved on to *développés.*

Don't think about Griff. Stay happy and calm. This is it. Your big day. You can do it. Happy and calm.

Fortunately, the day was a full one. After the warm-up class, there was another, final rehearsal where Oliver Damson, their artistic director, once again made certain that every element in the production was perfect.

Whenever Eva wasn't required on stage, she found a quiet place to remain alone while she visualised dancing her role perfectly. She pictured Juliet's first sighting of Romeo, and then the scenes with her nurse and the preparations for the ball. She imagined the balcony scene, and the Love Dance. Then the drama of the third act, with the beautiful scene with Romeo in Juliet's bedroom.

Eva did her best to remain deeply immersed

in the pathos of the young lovers' dilemma, but suddenly Griff was there again, intruding into her thoughts.

And this time he wouldn't leave. Eva was seeing him again, as her own young lover, and then as a mature and gorgeous, sexy man. The father of her child, the stirrer of her senses, the keeper of her heart.

Griff Fletcher was the source of her deepest angst but also the cause of her greatest happiness, and she'd run away from him. Again.

And suddenly, in the middle of the final rehearsal, Eva realised the truth she'd been avoiding.

I'm an idiot. I'm a total and utter fool.

With sudden and blinding certainty, she knew what she must do.

At some point in the ninety minutes that were set aside for the dancers to get into their costumes and to have their hair and make-up done, Eva had to make a very important phone call, and she had to find Oliver Damson and tell him she'd reached an important and final decision.

* * *

Although Griff had been to Paris before, he'd avoided visiting the Opéra de Paris. This evening, as he ascended the steps leading to this magnificent edifice, he could totally understand why the building was regarded as one of the world's greatest opera and ballet houses.

The exterior was elaborately decorated with angels and gargoyles and magnificent archways, but the interior was even more breathtaking. Here there were grand marble staircases, dazzling chandeliers, beautiful paintings on the ceilings and all manner of balustrades and balconies. And then, of course, in the inner sanctum stood the few square metres that all this pomp and grandeur were designed to complement— the stage.

The famous stage where Eva Hennessey, the girl from the tiny Aussie town of Emerald Bay, would dance her socks off.

Griff, in a brand new black dinner suit and bow tie, had never felt as nervous as he did now when he took his seat. Somewhere backstage, behind those grand velvet curtains, Eva was waiting. *His* Eva.

As he took his seat, his composure evaporated.

He tried to concentrate on the programme, wondering why on earth Eva had chosen a story about youthful, star-crossed lovers for her come-back. All Griff could think about was their own ill-fated romance and his new understanding of the blame he shared.

He turned to Eva's bio. The photo of her was a black and white head shot that showed off the slender elegance of her lovely neck and shoulders and made the contrast between her pale skin and dark hair even more dramatic than usual.

So beautiful.

Soon she would be on that stage in front of him, dancing.

Sweat broke out on Griff's brow and his collar felt too tight.

He closed the programme and willed himself to relax by watching the people in the audience as they filed into the theatre and took their seats. Glamorous Parisians in their finery were a very impressive bunch. He wondered how many of them ever gave a thought to Eva's background and her early life in a small beachside town in rural Australia.

He considered the huge effort Eva had put in to reach this place. Natural ability and talent could only take a dancer so far. The rest only came with punishing hard work and perseverance.

Eva had achieved so much. And Griff was miserably aware, even before the curtain rose, that he was crazy to imagine that she might ever want to leave this life.

Needless to say, it was an evening of extraordinary revelation for Griff. *Romeo and Juliet* had it all—swordplay, bawdy humour, romance and tragedy, all unfolding within a stunningly rich set design. The combination of Prokofiev's heart-rending music with the dancers' exquisite beauty and astonishing athleticism was enthralling. He hadn't expected to be so utterly enchanted and moved.

There were so many surprises. For one, he'd

been braced to see girls in tutus and pointe shoes, with their hair scraped into tight buns and accompanied by men in tights with ridiculous bulges.

Instead, these dancers were dressed in the richly brocaded costumes of the Italian Renaissance. For most of the ballet, Eva, as Juliet, wore a lovely calf-length dress in a soft, smoky pink fabric with a sleeveless bodice criss-crossed with bronze braid. And, instead of a bun, her hair was secured at the nape of her neck, then left to hang free in a silken river that reached halfway down her back.

She looked far more beautiful than Griff could have possibly imagined and, from his first sight of her, his gaze was riveted. He hardly dared to breathe.

She was so quick and graceful, so light on her feet, so utterly flawless and completely eye-catching in every sense of the word. And she was also deeply immersed in her role. Her look across the stage to Romeo had a completely new kind of bleakness that tore at Griff's soul.

No wonder she loved this work. No wonder the world adored her.

Eva was stunning, breathtaking. Griff wanted to kill her partner, with his male model looks, powerhouse physique and impeccable dancing technique. But Griff soon understood that it was the audience who were his main rivals.

When Eva took her bow at the end of the third act, the audience rose as one to applaud and cheer her and to throw bouquets onto the stage at her feet. The enthusiastic applause lasted for ages. Griff wasn't sure how long, but he feared he had his answer, and it wasn't the answer he'd hoped for.

There could be no doubt. This stage was where Eva belonged.

Eva was flushed and exhilarated as she returned to her dressing room, which was so crammed with flowers she could scarcely squeeze her way in.

She'd achieved what many had thought impossible. She'd danced as well tonight as she ever had, and she was satisfied.

Taking her seat before the mirror, she shoved

some of the flowers aside and began to remove the false eyelashes that looked good on stage but were so unnatural close up. Then she began with the special cleansing lotion she routinely used to remove the rest of her make-up.

This ritual was almost complete when she saw the small bunch of white daisies with a note attached. The daisies grabbed her attention first, because they were so different from the rest of the fancy roses and carnations and lilies.

Eva had always loved the simplicity of daisies. Griff had known this and he'd given them to her at their school formal—

Her thoughts froze as she saw the handwriting on the attached card. Her heart seemed to stop beating altogether and then it took a huge, fearful bound as she snatched up the flowers and read the note.

Here I am in Paris at the ballet. Sorry it's taken me so long.
Any chance of seeing you after the show?
G xx

Griff was here?

Any chance?

Eva was already leaping to her feet, knocking the chair sideways in her rush to get to the dressing room door. Her thoughts were racing as fast as her actions. Where would Griff be waiting? In the Foyer de la Danse? Would he find his way backstage? Would he know who to ask? If only she'd known he was coming, she could have made arrangements.

She flung the door open.

And there he was, coming down the corridor, looking drop-dead divine in formal black evening clothes.

Eva's heart thumped hard. She was trembling. She couldn't believe it really was Griff. Here in Paris.

'Hi,' she whispered as he came to a halt.

'Hi,' was all he said too.

She had to grip the door for support while her heart kept up its reckless thumping. Griff had come all this way and he looked amazing. So tall and broad-shouldered and smooth in his dinner jacket, but still with that rough, untidy hair that she loved. So gorgeous, in fact, that she couldn't think of any of the appropriate things to say.

She didn't thank him for the flowers, or ask him why he was here, or whether he'd enjoyed the show. He had, after all, just witnessed his first ballet performance, but she didn't ask Griff any of these questions.

Instead, she acted on instincts that had been too long suppressed. She launched recklessly forward, flinging her arms around his neck.

'It's so good to see you.'

Griff's arms encircled her. 'Damsel, you were amazing tonight.'

She pressed closer, wanting to bury her nose where his sun-bronzed neck showed above his stiff collar. 'I've missed you so much.'

'Truly, you were magnificent.'

Griff smelled so good. And he felt good too. So strong beneath his sleek, expensive suit. 'Oh, Griff.'

'There were so many things I wanted to tell you, but that was before I saw you tonight.'

They were talking at cross purposes. Griff was in danger of being overawed by all the fuss, while Eva was simply desperate to have his arms around her, his lips locked with hers.

Grabbing his hand, she drew him with her as she backed towards the open doorway of her dressing room. 'Come in.'

He didn't need a second invitation.

But once he was inside and the door was safely closed and surreptitiously locked, he looked around at the huge piles of flowers.

'Wow!'

Eva gave an impatient shake of her head. She didn't want to talk about the performance, or the audience's wonderful, over-the-top reception. None of that mattered now.

All she wanted was for Griff to kiss her. He wouldn't back off now. Surely, not after coming all this way?

'It's so good to see you,' she said again.

'You too.' Griff's grey eyes were bright and shiny.

Now, in the well-lit dressing room, she could see that he seemed a little shaken.

Perhaps this wasn't quite the moment to jump his bones as she longed to do.

'So now you've had your first taste of the ballet,' she said instead, as she righted the chair she'd knocked in her haste to find him. 'What did you think of it?'

For the first time Griff smiled, although his smile was still a little shaky. 'You want my honest opinion?'

'Sure,' she said bravely, although she didn't know what she would do if he'd hated it.

'I think I'm hooked.'

'Hooked on the ballet?' She couldn't help grinning like an eager child. 'You liked *Romeo and Juliet*?'

'I loved it.' Griff's smile was warm now and his eyes held that special light that caused all kinds of melting sensations inside her. 'Especially you, Eva. You were sensational.'

She was blushing. His praise meant so much to her.

'But I have to apologise,' Griff said next.

The change in his tone made her suddenly nervous. 'Why?'

'For taking so damned long to get here. I was jealous of your dancing. I never thought you could love me as much as you loved to dance. It's stupid, I know. I'm wiser now, I promise.'

Eva drew a sharp breath. This was such a big admission. Huge. She had no idea where it might take them but, right at this moment, it didn't seem to matter.

'Well, you're here now,' she said, stepping boldly forward and slipping her arms around him again. 'And you're not going to reject me now, are you?'

A soft sound, half-laugh, half-groan, escaped Griff, but he didn't back away. Better still, his hands came up to frame Eva's face as he leaned in to kiss her.

CHAPTER ELEVEN

DON'T RUSH THIS, Griff warned himself as his lips met Eva's. He was sure there were serious matters they needed to discuss before they got carried away, but right now he couldn't remember a single one of them. Good intentions hardly counted when Eva was pressing close, pushing her heavenly slender body against him in ways guaranteed to blitz his self-control.

Within seconds Griff was lost. Lost in the deliciousness and the smell and the feel of her. As his hands glided over her lovely limbs and under her dress, he was lost to desire too strong for restraint.

If there were correct protocols for theatre dressing rooms, they flew out of the window now. He and Eva had been waiting too long. Their passions were running too high. They were lovers reunited. Tonight there were no holds barred.

* * *

Later, they spent a scant ten minutes at the party in the Foyer de la Danse, where Eva politely acknowledged the enthusiasm of the special audience members who'd been invited to the after show supper.

She hoped she didn't look too excited and inordinately happy as she introduced Griff to Oliver Damson. In truth, she found it hard to concentrate on anything. She was too buzzy and elated. Too conscious of Griff's physical presence at her side. She kept wanting to touch him again.

Oliver looked Griff up and down and said, 'So you're the culprit, are you?'

Poor Griff was, of course, totally baffled.

'Griff has no idea what you're talking about,' Eva said, sending Oliver a warning frown.

'Hmm,' was Oliver's response, but then he offered them both a paternal smile. 'Off you go. Get home. Eva has another performance tomorrow night and she needs her beauty sleep.'

So he'd obviously guessed how madly in love

she was. Eva wondered how many others had noticed.

'What was all that about?' Griff asked when they were outside on the pavement, hailing a taxi. 'Why am I a culprit?'

'I can explain,' Eva told him. 'You'll come back to my place, won't you?'

'Is that an invitation?' he asked with a smile.

'Of course,' she said as a taxi pulled into the kerb and she gave the driver her address.

It seemed Griff was happy to accept and, once they were inside, sitting together on the back seat, Eva took his hand, as she'd been dying to do. 'You probably won't believe this, but tonight, just before the show, I told Oliver that I want to retire.'

Griff stared at her. 'But you've just worked your butt off to get back on stage. You were fantastic tonight.'

'Well, yes, I've achieved my goal, but tonight I also realised that it wasn't enough.'

'What do you want to do?' Griff sounded worried now.

Eva couldn't help grinning as she told him. 'Apart from giving the younger dancers their chance at stardom by stepping out of the way, I'm taking a job in Brisbane with Ballet Pacifique.'

'As a dancer?'

'No, as their artistic director. I was incredibly lucky. They offered me the job last November and I turned them down. Today, when I called back, they'd got down to the shortlist and were about to start interviews.'

'But they still want you?'

'Yes. I managed to hang onto the job of my dreams by the skin of my teeth.'

'Well done.'

Now it was Eva's turn to be worried. 'Are you pleased, Griff?'

'Yes, of course,' he said. 'Congratulations.'

But he was quiet as the taxi turned into her street and pulled up outside her apartment. He insisted on paying the fare and Eva, somewhat subdued, introduced him to Balzac, the concierge's glamorous grey cat, while they waited for the lift to arrive.

The lift made its way creakily upwards and Eva started to feel nervous again, uneasy about the pause in their conversation at a crucial moment. She unlocked the door to her apartment and flicked a switch that turned on lamps.

'Oh, Eva,' Griff said. 'This is beautiful.' He walked into the lounge room, looking about him at her paintings, at her carefully chosen furnishings. He stepped closer to study her collection of shells, and the piece of coral she'd found in Emerald Bay. Then he turned his attention to the lovely view of city lights, including the Eiffel Tower.

At last, he turned to her. 'Can you really give this up?'

Eva nodded. 'Of course.' It was only bricks and mortar, after all.

Griff seemed to need a moment to take this in. His chest rose and fell as he inhaled deeply, then let his breath out again.

'Would you like a drink?' Eva remembered her hostess duties. 'Scotch? Wine? Coffee?'

'What are you having?'

She smiled. 'Hot chocolate.'

Griff smiled too. 'I'll go for the Scotch, thanks.' He followed her into her tiny kitchen and watched as she fixed his drink and set a pot of milk on the stove.

'Would you like ice with this?'

'Just a little, thanks.' Griff's gaze was serious as he took the glass she offered. 'What made you change your mind about the Brisbane job?' he asked. 'I suppose you wanted to be closer to Laine.'

Eva was about to reach for the tin of powdered chocolate, but now she stopped and turned to him. 'Well, yes, being able to see Laine is a bonus. How is she, by the way? I can't believe I didn't ask earlier, but I guess I was a little distracted.'

This brought another smile from Griff. 'She's fighting fit. Claims she's the size of a hippopotamus, but she looks perfect to me.'

For Eva, the fact that their daughter was due to give birth any day now truly highlighted the significance of Griff's journey here to the other side of the world.

His gaze was serious again. 'Are you sure about giving up dancing, Eva? It's a huge step.'

She nodded. It was vitally important that she explained this properly and she had to choose her words carefully. 'It came to me during the final rehearsal. I was remembering a conversation you and I had, about wisdom and courage. I realised that taking a job in Brisbane wasn't just wise and sensible; it was where I really wanted to be. Then I realised that I was only staying away because I lacked courage. I was scared.'

'Scared?'

'Yes, I was scared to live there if you didn't love me.' Eva couldn't believe she'd been brave enough to say this.

When Griff opened his mouth to protest, she held up her hand. 'Tonight, before the show, it dawned on me that I was going to miss you, Griff, wherever I was. Even living here in a lovely and exciting city like Paris, I've missed you terribly, so, at least, if I was in the same city, I could see you from time to time.' She swallowed nervously. 'Even if you were only ever on the fringes of my life.'

'The fringes? Why would I be on the fringes?'

'Well, I wasn't sure, you see.'

'Oh, Eva.' Setting aside his glass, Griff reached for her. 'I love you. I don't know why it's taken me so long to tell you. I need you. I want you in the *centre* of my life, not on the fringes. I love you so much.'

Such a wonderful rush of relief swamped Eva, she might have melted back into his arms at that moment, but a hissing noise behind her reminded her of the milk on the stove. Quickly, she turned, switched it off and shifted the pot to a cooler spot.

Shyly, she smiled at Griff. 'Is that why you're here? To tell me that you love me?'

'Yes, but, to be honest, I was scared too. I didn't want to take you away from your dancing. I was looking into the possibility of getting some kind of work visa and brushing up on my French.'

'Oh, Griff.' She was overawed by the thought of him giving up everything for her. Slipping her arms around him, she kissed his jaw, where a five o'clock shadow was starting to show.

'I love you,' she murmured as she kissed her way from his jaw to his lips.

He was already there to meet her, his lips parting, his arms tightening around her, and happiness swum in Eva's veins as they let their kiss deepen at a leisurely pace. Their drinks abandoned, Griff drew Eva closer and they kissed and kissed, like teenagers. Or, rather, like adults who at last had the luxury to enjoy the lack of haste, to savour a slow, seductive intimacy, secure and confident at last in the love that had been waiting for them for so long.

CHAPTER TWELVE

LAINE AND DYLAN were married at the very end of winter. By that time, Eva had returned to Brisbane and baby Leo was four months old. He was a gorgeous, roly-poly little fellow, full of smiles, who easily won everyone's hearts, especially Eva's and Griff's.

The day of the wedding dawned bright and sunny, perfect for an outdoor wedding, with blue skies, only a few fluffy white clouds and clear sunshine that brought the first hints of spring.

At Dylan's family home in Brookfield, a big white marquee had been erected on a pristine lawn. Seating for the ceremony was arranged under a huge spreading jacaranda tree and the path leading to this area was bordered by palm trees in pots decorated with white satin bows and white and silver balloons.

'Dylan's family have gone all out with the preparations,' Laine had told Eva and Griff, and now the stage was clearly set for a joyous occasion.

'Come a bit early,' Laine had also told Eva. 'I'll be getting dressed at Dylan's parents' house. It saves any worries about traffic and trying to get to the wedding on time, and it's a better venue for the photographer. I'd really love to see you before I walk down the aisle.'

Eva was touched by the invitation.

'I'll be in a little studio out the back of the house,' Laine added. 'And Dylan won't be allowed to get so much as a glimpse of me.'

Eva wore her grey silk dress, rather than buying anything new. She was very aware that this was Ruth Templeton's day to shine as mother of the bride, and she was prepared to stay very much in the background.

Eva's main task today, she'd decided, was to keep a check on her emotions. She was so very conscious that, in her family, Laine would be the first woman in three generations to marry her baby's father. The first to provide her child with the security of a complete family unit. Eva was immensely proud of Laine and so very happy for her and Dylan.

'Wow!' Griff said when he saw her dressed for the wedding.

Eva had chosen silver accessories to complement the grey silk and she'd pulled her hair into a low chignon with a pink rosebud tucked into it.

'You haven't brushed up too badly, yourself,' she told him, eyeing his beautifully cut charcoal suit and stylish grey and silver tie.

They shared happy smiles. It was almost as if they'd planned their outfits to match. As if they were meant to—

Don't, Eva warned herself. *Don't get too nostalgic today.*

She and Griff were blissfully happy and she had absolutely no doubt that her return to Brisbane had been the right decision. Annoyingly, the mistakes of her past still had the power to haunt her, but today her eyes were on the future and not on the past and the years that they'd lost.

Today she had to stay completely focused on Laine and Dylan. This was all about them.

When Eva and Griff arrived, they were greeted by Dylan's father, who was dressed rather grandly in a formal suit for the wedding, while happily sporting a towel over his shoulder to catch any dribbles from the grandson in his arms.

'Welcome, welcome,' he said, all beaming smiles, and he immediately offered Griff a calming snifter of Scotch.

'Would you like my help with the baby?' Eva offered, holding out her arms in readiness.

'Later, not now.' Her jovial host gave a wave of his hand towards the back of the house. 'I believe there's a bride out there who's expecting you.'

'Oh, lovely. Yes, of course.'

Eva found Laine, just as her daughter had promised, in a small garden studio at the back of the main house.

Although it was Ruth Templeton who met her at the door.

'Ruth,' Eva said. 'How lovely you look.'

Ruth was dressed in a crimson two piece suit and her normally limp grey hair had been curled and carefully styled. Her face was glowing with excitement. 'Thank you.' Her joyous smile broadened. 'I wanted to wear something bright and cheerful on such a happy day.'

'That colour's perfect on you,' Eva told her.

Eyes wide, Ruth nodded towards the studio's interior. 'Wait till you see our girl.'

Our girl. Eva hadn't expected to be so generously included and she felt the sting of tears.

No. Not now. She had to stay strong. Heaven knew she was used to putting on a performance face.

But then she saw Laine.

Oh, my goodness.

Her daughter was breathtakingly beautiful. Already Laine was almost back to her pre-pregnancy slimness and her wedding dress, made of exquisite filigree lace, was cleverly cut to flatter her slightly changed figure.

Laine's dark hair was gleaming with health.

The purple streaks had grown out and a fresh, new wispy cut framed her face perfectly. Her complexion was flawless and glowing and her headdress was a simple, elegant arrangement of white flowers pinned into her hair. Laine smiled at Eva and her grey eyes were shining with happiness and excitement, and with irrepressible joy.

'Oh, Laine.'

It was all Eva could manage before her throat became painfully choked.

'She's going to blow Dylan away, isn't she?' Ruth said, still smiling broadly.

'Yes, absolutely,' Eva agreed, although she was also wondering how Griff would react when he saw his beautiful grown-up daughter.

'Thanks, both of you, darlings.' Laine hugged them carefully, so as not to smudge her make-up, before the photographer took photos of the three of them in different poses and combinations. Then Laine crossed the room to collect her bridal bouquet from a box on the table.

She was halfway across the room when it happened.

One minute she was fine, moving easily and confidently. Then she stumbled and let out a cry.

Eva's heart leapt high.

'Laine!' cried Ruth.

Both women rushed to her aid.

Luckily, Laine didn't fall, but she was reaching down to remove one of her glamorous silk-sheathed, high heeled shoes. With a look of dismay, she held it up. The slender heel had snapped.

'Oh!' cried a horrified Ruth. 'Oh, Laine, no! How can that have happened? What can we do?'

'I don't know.' The poor girl looked utterly forlorn as she stared at the sleek satin shoe with its snapped, dangling heel. In a blink she'd been transformed from an excited, hopeful and beautiful bride into a picture of utter dismay.

'Did you bring any spare shoes?' asked Ruth.

Laine gave a doleful shake of her head. 'I only have my blue sneakers. Not a great look for a bride.' She pushed the snapped heel back into place. 'I wonder if we can fix this… Maybe Dylan's parents have some superglue.'

'Oh, I don't think that's a good idea.' Ruth sounded frantic and she was madly looking about her, as if a miracle might materialise out of thin air. 'I know I'd spend the whole wedding on tenterhooks, waiting for your heel to snap again.'

Anxiously, Ruth looked down at her own feet. 'I'd lend you my shoes if I could, but my feet are too wide. You'd walk right out of them. And black's the wrong colour for you, anyway.'

'I'm afraid I'm no help.' The photographer pointed to his black leather lace-up boots with a rueful smile.

'Try mine,' said Eva, quickly slipping off a shoe.

Laine gave a huff of surprise. 'But—'

'Go on,' Eva said, holding out the silver shoe. 'You never know—it might fit.'

'But what about you? What will you wear?'

Eva gave a shrugging smile. 'I have ballet flats in my handbag. Ever since I had trouble with my hip, I've carried them as a safety precaution. So if these shoes fit you, you're very welcome to them. We can't send you off as a barefoot bride.'

'Wow, thanks,' said Laine.

'You should probably sit down to try them on.'

Laine did this, sitting carefully on the edge of a chair in her elegant lacy gown. The two mothers and the photographer all held their breath as she fitted her foot into the shoe.

'I think it fits,' Laine said in a cautious stage whisper, as if she didn't want to tempt fate.

'Oh, thank heavens,' breathed Ruth. 'Try the other one.'

Eva handed the second shoe over and Laine slipped it on. As she did so, Eva noticed again the butterfly birthmark on her daughter's ankle and her thoughts flashed straight back to the day of her baby's birth and her first sight of that tiny, memorable mark. For a dangerous moment, Eva felt tears threaten again.

She was saved by Ruth's intense command.

'Stand up now, Laine. See if you can walk in them.'

Obediently, Laine stood, then walked, gingerly at first and then more confidently. 'They do fit!' she cried excitedly. 'They're perfect.'

She shot Eva a look of joyful surprise. 'We must have exactly the same-sized feet.' Then, with a wondrous smile, she looked down at her feet, peeping from beneath the hem of her white silk gown. 'And the silver looks so pretty.'

'Then you're very welcome to them,' said Eva as she slipped on the black ballet flats.

Laine now looked at Eva's feet and frowned. 'Are you sure?'

'Absolutely. Of course I'm sure, darling.'

Eva had never been surer of anything. For the first time in twenty years, she had been able to perform one small motherly gesture for her daughter, and the tiny act filled her with intense satisfaction.

To her surprise, Ruth Templeton hugged her. 'Thank you, Eva,' the other woman said fervently. 'Thank you for the shoes, and thank you for giving us our beautiful daughter.'

Eva couldn't speak. Her heart was too full. She was glowing with over-the-top joy. For the first time, she could finally look at the adoption as a happy gift instead of a painful sacrifice. She saw the silver glitter of tears in Ruth's eyes and felt her own eyes well up.

'Hey, don't start bawling, you two!' ordered their daughter. 'I don't want two blubbering mothers.'

It was the warning the women needed, bringing them back from the brink. Instead of weeping, they shared wobbly smiles and then a shy laugh, just as Ruth's husband, Donald, appeared in the studio's doorway.

'I do believe there's a beautiful bride in here,' Donald said, grinning.

'There is, indeed,' Laine told him triumphantly. 'And she now has two shoes and she's waiting impatiently to be married.'

Griff frowned when he saw Eva in her ballet flats instead of the silver heels. 'Is your hip hurting?' he asked with concern.

'No,' Eva assured him and she explained about

Laine's last-minute heel catastrophe. 'I lent her my silver shoes. They fitted her perfectly.'

She smiled at him. She was feeling so much better now. Calmer and happier, and relieved to throw off at least some of the guilt from her past, and to look forward instead to an ongoing loving relationship with Laine, Dylan and Leo. But she wondered how Griff would feel when he saw his daughter as a beautiful bride, and watched her walking down the aisle on another man's arm.

'I've been so worried about weeping all over the place today,' she told him. 'But I think I have a plan. Whenever I feel mopey, I'll just focus on those silver shoes and pray that the heels hold.'

Griff smiled and reached for her hand. 'Sounds like an excellent plan.' His warm fingers wrapped around hers and he squeezed her hand gently. 'I might adopt it too. Come, let's watch our kid get married.'

The wedding was an all-round happy occasion, as lovely as everyone had hoped it would be.

Dylan's shiny-eyed smile as he watched Laine walking towards him had everyone melting, and the young couple's vows were beautifully sincere.

The reception in the marquee was relaxed and friendly. The other guests didn't know the significance of Eva and Griff's relationship to the happy couple, and if they were asked they merely said they were friends of the bride.

After the bridal waltz, Laine danced with Donald Templeton, and Eva and Griff were happy to watch on. But then, to their surprise, Laine crossed the dance floor and beckoned to Griff.

'Go on,' Eva whispered when he hesitated.

Laine was holding out her hand with a special smile just for Griff, and Eva's heart filled her throat as he rose and walked to their daughter. As Griff and Laine began to dance, Eva almost allowed the poignancy of the moment to touch her too deeply, but she focused on the shoes, her silver shoes.

She had spent decades as a professional ballerina and yet she knew this simple waltz on a temporary wooden floor would stay locked in her memory till the end of her days.

CHAPTER THIRTEEN

As a brilliant sun rose over the eastern rim of Emerald Bay, the household on the clifftop was stirring.

Twelve-month-old Leo woke first and crawled to the edge of his cot, where he grabbed at the bars and pulled himself up to stand on sturdy, chubby legs. When his first cry penetrated the morning stillness, Laine stirred in the next room.

'I'll get him,' Dylan said, slipping quickly out of their bed.

'Bless you.' Laine adored her beautiful baby boy but she'd also developed an enormous gratitude for the enthusiasm with which her husband viewed fatherhood. Now, she happily pulled the sheet over her head and snuggled down for a few extra minutes of precious peace.

Down the hallway in the main bedroom, Griff

heard the baby's cry and woke. Almost immediately, Eva was stirring beside him. After an entire year, he still considered it a miracle to wake and find her beside him each morning. Now, he watched her eyes open slowly and saw the flash of aqua blue that had first bewitched him way back in high school.

'Morning,' she murmured sleepily, pressing her lips to his bare shoulder.

'Morning.' He kissed the tip of her nose. For a few minutes they lay, listening to the sounds of the sea and the gulls calling.

Eva yawned and stretched. 'I might go and get Leo.'

'I think Dylan's beaten you to it.'

'Oh.' She smiled. 'My turn tomorrow morning then.'

'Fancy an early morning swim?' Griff asked.

Her eyes flashed wide with interest, but then she pulled a face. 'I promised I'd do omelettes for breakfast.'

'We'd still have time for a quick dip.'

She grinned. 'Why not?' Already she was sitting up, throwing off the sheet and swinging her slim legs over the edge of the bed.

Suppressing the urge to roll her straight back onto the mattress, Griff went to fetch their bathers from the balcony where they'd been left to dry.

They'd bought this house at Emerald Bay six months ago and it had quickly proved to be a wonderful getaway—the perfect counterpoint to their busy city lives. At Christmas, with the addition of a couple of caravans parked in the yard, it would also be the perfect venue for a happy family gathering that would include Eva's mother and her husband, as well as the Templetons and Laine, Dylan and little Leo, who everyone agreed was a ripper of a kid.

Tomorrow Griff's parents would be arriving for one of their regular visits. To Griff's delight, they'd embraced Eva and their daughter and her family with reassuring warmth.

'It's so much more peaceful at your place than it is at Julia's with her tribe,' his mother had confided. 'And Emerald Bay is so beautiful.'

True. This morning the view from their bedroom showed the autumn day was dawning fresh and clear, with a nice clean wave breaking onshore. Eva, looking incredibly youthful and slim, with a baggy old T-shirt over her bikini, grinned at Griff.

'Race you to the surf,' she dared, and then with a laugh, and without waiting while he gathered up their towels, was off, out of the door and over the lawn, down the stone steps that had been cut into the side of the cliff.

She had reached the bottom and was skirting the rocky headland at the end of the beach when she saw the bright flash of blue that stopped her.

'What is it?' Griff called as he caught up.

'Look!' She pointed to a small pool hollowed out of the rock. 'Look what's here.'

Coming closer, Griff saw, swimming in the clear basin of seawater, a small, perfect, bright blue fish with an even brighter yellow tail.

'A damsel,' he said softly.

'Yes. She must have washed in here with the tide. Isn't she beautiful?'

'Amazingly so.'

They stood together, watching the little fish circle the pond, slightly awed by their discovery.

'I'd hate to think she was going to be stuck here,' Eva said. 'But she'll leave again with the next high tide, won't she?'

'Yes.' Griff nodded and then he looked away, as if an unpleasant thought had struck him.

'What?' Eva asked. 'What's the matter?'

'Nothing.' He gave a careless shrug.

But Eva, with the new perceptiveness she'd gained from living side by side with this man, guessed the cause of his frown and she reached for his hand. 'I won't be leaving you again, Griff.'

'No, I know you won't.'

'You believe me, don't you?'

He was smiling now but, despite the smile, she saw that soul-deep look in his eyes that she remembered from so long ago.

'I promise, Griff.'

'That's good to know,' he said lightly. 'Because

I was about to suggest that it's time we followed our daughter's good example and got married.'

Eva gasped, rendered suddenly breathless by shock and delight. Then a small, laughing huff escaped her. 'I thought you'd never ask.'

'I'm asking you now, Damsel.'

And indeed he was. Standing on the rocky headland where they'd once shared their first kiss, Griff took both of her hands in his. 'Will you do me the huge honour of becoming my wife?'

'Yes, please!'

The little blue fish completed yet another circuit of its tiny pond and Eva, with a shriek of unfettered joy, leapt into the arms of the one and only man who could make her world right.

* * * * *

MILLS & BOON®
Large Print – August 2017

The Italian's One-Night Baby
Lynne Graham

The Desert King's Captive Bride
Annie West

Once a Moretti Wife
Michelle Smart

The Boss's Nine-Month Negotiation
Maya Blake

The Secret Heir of Alazar
Kate Hewitt

Crowned for the Drakon Legacy
Tara Pammi

His Mistress with Two Secrets
Dani Collins

Stranded with the Secret Billionaire
Marion Lennox

Reunited by a Baby Bombshell
Barbara Hannay

The Spanish Tycoon's Takeover
Michelle Douglas

Miss Prim and the Maverick Millionaire
Nina Singh

MILLS & BOON®
Large Print – September 2017

The Sheikh's Bought Wife
Sharon Kendrick

The Innocent's Shameful Secret
Sara Craven

The Magnate's Tempestuous Marriage
Miranda Lee

The Forced Bride of Alazar
Kate Hewitt

Bound by the Sultan's Baby
Carol Marinelli

Blackmailed Down the Aisle
Louise Fuller

Di Marcello's Secret Son
Rachael Thomas

Conveniently Wed to the Greek
Kandy Shepherd

His Shy Cinderella
Kate Hardy

Falling for the Rebel Princess
Ellie Darkins

Claimed by the Wealthy Magnate
Nina Milne

MILLS & BOON®

Why shop at millsandboon.co.uk?

Each year, thousands of romance readers find their perfect read at millsandboon.co.uk. That's because we're passionate about bringing you the very best romantic fiction. Here are some of the advantages of shopping at www.millsandboon.co.uk:

* **Get new books first**—you'll be able to buy your favourite books one month before they hit the shops

* **Get exclusive discounts**—you'll also be able to buy our specially created monthly collections, with up to 50% off the RRP

* **Find your favourite authors**—latest news, interviews and new releases for all your favourite authors and series on our website, plus ideas for what to try next

* **Join in**—once you've bought your favourite books, don't forget to register with us to rate, review and join in the discussions

Visit **www.millsandboon.co.uk**
for all this and more today!